Falling for a Drug Dealer
Part 2
-A Story Written by-
Melikia Gaino

Copyright © 2015 by True Glory Publications
Published by True Glory Publications LLC
Facebook: Melikia Gaino
Join our Mailing list by texting TrueGlory at 95577

This story is a work of fiction. Any resemblances to actual events, real people, living or dead, organizations, establishments or locales are products of the author's imagination. Other names, characters, places, and incidents are used fictitiously.

Cover Design: Michael Horne
Editor: Kylar Bradshaw

Because of the dynamic nature of the Internet, any Web addresses or links contained in this book may have changed since publication, and may no longer be valid. The views expressed in this work are solely those of the author and do not necessarily reflect the views of the publisher and the publisher hereby disclaims any responsibility for them.

Acknowledgements

First and foremost, I would like to thank my Lord and Savior, Jesus Christ, for given me the strength and creative mind to write what I have. I cannot wait to see where this road takes me and what else He has in store for me. I'm more than nervous about venturing out into the world of writing, but I have faith that the road traveled will be a great one. Where there is faith there should be no worry.

I would like to thank the Gaino and Williams/Mabry family for their love and support and never letting me give up on a dream. I LOVE YOU ALL!!!

I would also like to thank you the readers for supporting me on my first book and taking the time to read one of my favorite creations.

Table of Contents

Chapter 1   1

Chapter 2   7

Chapter 3   12

Chapter 4   15

Chapter 5   20

Chapter 6   26

Chapter 7   31

Chapter 8   35

Chapter 9   39

Chapter 10   44

Chapter 11   50

Chapter 12   55

Chapter 13   62

Chapter 14   67

Chapter 15   71

Chapter 16   79

Chapter 17   84

Chapter 18   89

Chapter 19   92

Chapter 20   98

Chapter 21   101

Chapter 22   107

Epilogue   114

True Glory Links   117

Falling for a Drug Dealer

Part II

When the shit hit the fan!!!!!

Chapter 1

Lisa

It's been three months and Lisa and Terence became the closest friends ever. Terence helped Lisa get her mother in a rehab center. He became Lisa's go-to-man anytime she needed someone to talk to. Lisa was in the house on a Thursday night studying a case for her job, when her phone rang.

"Hello." Lisa said.

"Hey boo. I ain't hear from you in a while." Lisa recognized the voice right away as Darnell's.

"Oh. Hey Darnell, what's up?" Lisa asked. Even though she attended church every Sunday, she tried to avoid Darnell because she still didn't feel comfortable around him.

"Nothing boo. You ain't been trying to talk to me in church or call me. What's up with that?" Darnell asked.

"Well, I haven't been trying to be around you because ever since that time we went out, I don't feel comfortable being around you. I feel like you tried to take advantage of me." Lisa said.

"That's bull shit. You knew you wanted it and I gave you what you wanted. You're a grown ass woman and ain't trying to let a nigga hit that. I should have taken it." Darnell said.

"I can't believe you just said that." Lisa said.

"I really didn't want to take your ass out anyway, all I wanted was some pussy." Darnell said.

1

"You know what Darnell, fuck you." Lisa said before she hung up the phone.

Lisa was so fucked up about what Darnell just said to her that she needed to call somebody. She called the first person that she knew she could talk too.

"Hey baby, what's up?" Terence said once he noticed Lisa's number on his caller id.

"I need someone to talk to." Lisa said on the verge of crying.

"What is it sweet heart? Is it your mother?" Terence asked knowing the relationship between Lisa and her mother.

"No not this time. Darnell just called."

"What did that nigga say to my baby?"

"He told me the only reason he ever took me out was so he could get some pussy."

"What? Where this nigga live? I'm going to fuck that fake ass pimp up." Terence said aggravated.

"Don't worry about it. He'll get his." Lisa didn't want Terence to hurt Darnell because if anything happened to him she would feel guilty.

"Are you ok, baby? I'm on my way to your house." Terence said before he hung up.

An half an hour later, Terence was at Lisa door.

"That was quick." Lisa said when she opened the door and saw Terence.

"I was out handling some business and came right over."

"What do you do for a living Terence? You never told me. You know everything about me, but I don't know anything about your life style." Lisa asked.

"Sweet heart if I let you know about my life style, that is a commitment to me that you would be in my life forever and you would be my woman not just my friend." Terence said so serious. He had been feeling Lisa and wanted her to be his woman, but she just wanted to be friends and he respected that.

Lisa looked Terence in the eyes and said, "I want to be with you and only you. You were there for me when no one else was and I love you."

The 'I love you' caught Terence by surprise, but he felt the same way about Lisa. "I love you too, Lisa."

Terence walked over to Lisa and picked her up and carried her to her room. When they got to the room, Terence placed Lisa on the bed softly and took her clothes off piece by piece. Then he removed his clothes. He stood in front of her naked and admired her naked body. Lisa looked down at him and tried breathing regularly. She saw how well-endowed Terence was and hoped that they fit. He turned on the stereo system to put on Maxwell's CD. The mood was set; he wanted everything to be perfect for her first time.

Terence walked back towards the bed. He gently pushed Lisa's legs apart and entered her slowly. The head of his penis was inside of her when he felt her tense up. She gasped sharply from the sudden surprise.

"Am I hurting you, baby?" Terence asked with deep concern. He kept his lower body motionless as to not cause any more pain to her.

"No, please don't stop." Lisa replied with tears falling from her eyes.

Terence looked at her unwillingly but couldn't help but admire her. He knew Lisa had waited all her life to share her body with someone she loved and he felt even happier to know that it was him.

While pleasing her with gentle strokes, he placed soft, passionate kisses over her face to help soothe her pain. When she couldn't take it anymore, he got off of her and said, "We can continue when you're ready, ma." He held her while she calmed down, being a gentlemen about the situation.

After twenty minutes passed, she told him, "I'm ready."

He got back on top of her and entered her more roughly and deeper. He was entering her with long, deep strokes until her legs started trembling uncontrollably, letting him know she was cumming.

He felt the contractions of her pussy, squeezing and pulling on his dick. They both ended up cumming together, him not being able to hold out any longer. Afterwards, he held her while she fell asleep in his arms.

The next morning when they woke up, he asked Lisa to take the day off from her job and spend the day with him. She agreed cause she was sore and wanted to spend more time with him.

"So after I give you a nice, warm bubble bath, we can get our day started baby." Terence said while looking at her. He

4

didn't want to admit it right then and there, but he felt himself falling for her.

"A bubble bath, huh?" Lisa replied sexily. "Are you joining me in the tub? It has room for two."

"Hmmm, you tryna tempt a brother into doing some things, but this bath is going to be for you. Imma wash you up and make sure I don't miss any areas."

Terence went into the connecting bathroom and began to run the water. Lisa could hear him moving about and slowly laid her head on the pillow.

'This feels like a dream or at least something you read in a book.' She thought to herself.

Before she could close her eyes, she felt herself being lifted off the bed into Terence's strong arms. She laid her head on his chest and wrapped her arms around his neck, savoring the moment. He placed her on her feet once they were inside the bathroom. She bent down to feel the water and smiled to herself.

"I've never had anybody run a bubble bath for me. Your making me blush and I rarely even do that." Lisa said.

"A woman like you deserves special treatment. You should know that." Terence replied.

After Terence gave Lisa a bubble bath, she would never forget, they went to the kitchen to eat breakfast and map out their day.

"Have you ever been to Tyson's corner?" Terence asked Lisa.

"I've been a couple of times, but I only go when I take my brother school shopping for clothes and shoes. Why you ask?"

"Well I figure we go out there ya know, do a little shopping, and buy a few things." Terence said.

"Shopping? What do you do for a living that you can just drop everything and take a girl shopping?" Lisa asked.

"Right now, all I can tell you is that I run the streets. That's all you need to know, ma."

"Oh Wow! I'm dating a drug dealer. This is crazy. What happens if you get locked up or worse, killed? What am I supposed to do if that happens? Why are you putting me in this predicament, Terence?" Lisa said on the brink of tears.

"Don't even think like that Lisa. Ain't shit gonna happen to me. That's why I didn't want to tell you cause I knew you would worry. You my woman now and I ain't never gonna leave you." He said while leaning over to kiss her.

They both got dressed and walked out of the house, prepared to start their day together.

Chapter 2

Kim

Kim was now five months pregnant and everything was going well with her and Shawn. Kim was home off of work and lying next to Shawn.

"Hey ma, why you up so early?" He asked feeling her move around.

"I don't know, just couldn't sleep." Kim said.

"Well come give your man some since you can't sleep." Shawn said.

Kim climbed on top of Shawn and rode him like he had never been ridden. He then laid her on her back and climbed on top. Once he got on top, he took his time and made love to Kim as if this was his last time ever being between her legs. While they made love he kept looking at her. Then they both climaxed together.

"Kim." Shawn said while she slept peaceful in his arms.

"Yes." Kim answered softly.

"I love you. You know that right?"

"Yes I know that and I love you too. You are scaring me Shawn. What's wrong?" Kim said now feeling worried.

"Ain't nothing wrong. Go back to sleep, ma. I'm about to hit the streets." Shawn said before he got up and took a shower.

When Shawn got out of the shower, he gave Kim a passionate kiss and left. Kim didn't think nothing of it and went back to sleep.

Ring, ring, ring...

"Hello." Kim said.

"Hey girl, wake up." London said through the phone.

"I'm up what's up?" Kim said with her eyes still closed.

"We all are going over to Lisa's house at 5:00. Do you need a ride?" London asked.

"Naw, I don't need a ride. I'll be there. Why are we all going over here?"

"Lisa said she has something to tell us." London said.

"Ok, I'll be there then." Kim said.

Once she got off the phone with London, she got up and got dressed and headed to Lisa's house.

When she got to Lisa's house, everybody was there, even Danni.

"So where you been Ms.?" London asked Lisa.

"I have been with my man." Lisa said with a smile and blushing.

"Your man?" Everyone said at the same time.

"Yes my man and I had sex." Lisa said.

Lisa filled the girls in and everyone was shocked, but they were happy for their girl.

"I'm so happy for you boo, but I'm sleepy so I'm going home. I love y'all." Kim said to her friends and left.

On the ride home Kim felt weird, but she shook off the feeling. When she walked in the house it was the same way as she left it. She walked to the kitchen to get some juice and when she walked in there she saw a letter on the fridge. She took the letter off the fridge and sat at the table to read it.

Dear Kim,

I love you, but I have to leave you. I know this some fucked up shit, but this is the only way you and my baby can be safe. I can't tell you where I'm going or where I will be. Don't cry baby girl because I will be back, but I don't want you to stop living because of me either. I know you going to live your life and I love you and my unborn child. I will be back, please don't be mad at me.

Love you always,

Shawn

Kim was shocked, hurt, and didn't know what to do, so she went to her phone and called Lisa's house where all the girls were at.

"Hello." Larry answered the phone.

"Can you put Lisa on the phone?" Kim said barely getting it out because she was crying so hard.

"Hello." Lisa said once she got on the phone.

"Lisa… he… left me." Kim said crying.

"Hold on baby girl. Who left you?" Lisa asked.

"Shawn left me and I'm pregnant. I'm having his fucking baby and he left me." Kim started crying harder because reality hit her.

"We on our way over there." Lisa said before hanging up the phone.

Kim hung up the phone and went to her bedroom; she felt like her life was over. All she could hear was her brother's voice in her head, *"What you going to do when he leaves you?"*

Kim's phone rang and she answered it because she thought it would be Shawn, but it was Malik.

"Baby girl, why are you crying?" Malik asked.

"He left me and I don't feel like being bothered, Malik, so please don't say anything."

"I won't do that, baby girl. I'm here for you. Get some rest and I'll be over there later." Malik said not liking the fact that his sister was hurting.

"I want to be alone. I'll call you when I want you to come over." Kim said.

"Ok, baby girl I respect that. I love you."

"Love you too, Malik." Kim hung up the phone and then she heard her front door open.

All of her friends walked in her room.

"Where the fuck is this motherfucking letter?" Tracey asked heated.

Kim just pointed to the nightstand, where she placed the letter. They all read it and all of them got angry and wanted to fuck some shit up, except Lisa.

"Maybe he left because someone would have hurt you and the baby to get to him." Lisa said.

"Fuck that, don't you think if they would hurt them to get to him while he is here. They would do it while he is not here." India said.

All the talk about Shawn put Kim in a deeper sorrow. So she zoned out while they talked. After a while, Kim fell asleep and the girls got ready to leave, but they didn't think Kim would be safe in that home by herself, so they called her cousin Jasmine to come over and keep an eye on her. When Jasmine came over the group of friends left.

Chapter 3

Tracey

Tracey walked in the house and smelled the food being cooked. She followed the smell to the kitchen and saw Kenny.

"Hey baby, that smells good, what are you cooking?" Tracey said giving Kenny a kiss.

"Oh yeah, it's your favorite baby. I just wanted to do something special for you." Kenny said.

"Oh that's so sweet. It's been a long day too."

"Well, sit down and tell me all about it." Kenny said, while he massaged her shoulders.

"My day started off fine, then out of nowhere, I had a load of work. I went to check on Kim and she's not doing very well." Tracey expressed her concern about her friend Kim.

"Kim's still down. I hope baby girl get it together before she put the baby in danger." Kenny said aware of Kim's situation.

"Yeah, I know."

"So tell me, Tracey, when are you going to have my baby?" Kenny said catching Tracey off of guard.

"I'm not having any children. My friends are having children, so I won't have to have any." Tracey said serious.

"Well, we just going to have to see about that. Because I want children and you will be my baby's mother." Kenny said.

Tracey just looked at him because she never saw this aggressive side of him and she liked it. She liked it so much it turned her on. Tracey looked at Kenny with a sexy look and said, "Well, I love when you get aggressive."

Kenny knew what time it was and said, "Well, if you like it so much, come over here and show me how much you like it."

Tracey walked over to Kenny and unbuckled his pants, and then she kneeled down and put his penis in her mouth. Tracey was sucking Kenny off so good that his knees started to buckle and he felt weak. After a while of Tracey's bomb ass head, Kenny couldn't hold out any longer and he came all in her mouth. Like a pro, Tracey swallowed it all.

Out of nowhere Kenny picked Tracey up and placed her on the table. He wasn't going to let Tracey just bitch him like that. So once she was on the table, he pulled her clothes off roughly and then he rammed his hard dick into her wet pussy. He was rough, but Tracey loved it. She loved a man to rough her up when they had sex. That turned Tracey on so much that she came back to back, multiple times. Kenny was enjoying the pleasure of being inside of Tracey unprotected, that he knew for sure that he was going to bust in her and she would end up pregnant with his baby.

When Tracey felt him tense up, she looked at Kenny and said, "Don't even think about it. You better pull out."

As soon as the words left her mouth, Kenny pulled out and bust on her stomach.

While Kenny finished preparing dinner, Tracey went upstairs to take a shower. When she got out of the shower, dinner was prepared and she sat down and ate with her man, then the phone rang.

"Hello." Kenny said when he answered the phone.

"Hey Kenny, can I speak to Tracey?" Lorren said. Kenny passed her the phone and smacked her ass hard.

"Hello." Tracey said, while rolling her eyes at Kenny.

"Hey girl, I need a favor." Lorren said.

"What's up girl?" Tracey asked.

"Can you watch RJ for me for tomorrow? I can't do this anymore with Rico, so I need to go and find me a place to live. I have a couple of appointments to view some apartments and I can't take him with me. I would ask London but she always… well that's another story. I called Lisa and India and they both have something to do, and Kim she still down." Lorren explained.

"You don't have to explain to me, hun. I'll watch little man." Tracey said.

Kenny sat there listening to the whole story and when Tracey got off the phone he said, "You can watch RJ, but don't want to have one of your own."

Tracey wasn't in the mood, so she just continued to eat and when she was done she went to her room and went to sleep.

Chapter 4

Lorren

"I can't take this shit anymore! I have to get away from this crazy fucker." Lorren said to herself as she got off the phone with Tracey.

Lorren was in the house all day other than when she went to school. When Rico came home, he started to fuss and bitch to Lorren about how she could have cleaned up the house since all she did was go to school. The house was clean and Rico had a deal that went wrong, so he took his anger out on Lorren. He went on and on about how she was lazy, a piece of shit, and some more bullshit. Lorren just knew she had to get away from him and she needed to do it fast.

The next morning, Lorren got up early as she always did so that she can drop RJ off and make it to work on time. She did her normal tasks, so Rico wouldn't think anything of her actions. After dropping RJ off at Tracey's house, Lorren headed to work to clock in. After she clocked in, she headed right back out to go and view the first apartment.

Lorren wasn't an apartment type person, but she would live in one to get away from Rico. Lorren always lived in a house and she could afford a house, but she would rather have an apartment.

The first apartment that Lorren went to see was in a bad neighborhood. She couldn't see herself or her son living in such neighborhood.

The second neighborhood was nice, but the apartment was little and she was looking for somewhere Rico couldn't find her.

Lorren was about to give up when she remembered that she had one more apartment to see. She drove out to Bowie. When she arrived at the apartment complex, she was happy that it looked beautiful. When she saw it, she was happy it was big, spacious, and perfect for her and RJ. She decided to sign the lease and called the furniture place to buy a new bed for her and RJ, a couch, and a TV. She was buying everything because she wanted to move in no later than that weekend. After everything was settled with the moving arrangements, she went back to work.

Later on that night...

Lorren walked in the house with RJ who was sleep. Rico was not home yet, so Lorren went to RJ's room and started packing his stuff up. She was moving fast because she didn't want Rico to know what she was doing. When she was done with RJ things, she started with her stuff. When she packed something, she would take the packed items in the guest room where she knew Rico would never go. A majority of her things were packed by the time that Rico made it home.

"Hey baby!" Rico said to Lorren when he walked in the room.

"Hey." Lorren replied back with no emotion at all.

"What's wrong with you? A nigga come in here trying to show his girl some love and you act like you don't love a nigga or something." Rico said.

"There is nothing wrong with me, I'm just tired and I do love you, Rico." Lorren said.

"Well, are you going to show me some love?"

16

"Naw, I'm not in the mood, maybe tomorrow." Lorren said not in the mood to have sex.

"So a nigga come home and can't get any from his woman when he wants it. That's some mothafucking bullshit."

"Well, it's just going to have to be some bullshit today because I'm tired and want to go to sleep." Lorren said because she knew if she had sex with Rico she would not leave.

Rico didn't want to hear the shit that Lorren was talking. He knew that Lorren wanted it because she always put on a chase as if she didn't want him, then he would pull her close to him and she would be all up on him.

Rico walked over to the bed where Lorren had pulled the covers up and got comfortable in the bed. He yanked the covers off of her and turned her on her back. Once she was on her back, he pulled her underwear to the side and he ate her out. Rico was flicking his tongue so well that Lorren came around five times. Her legs were shaking and her body was jerking. When he saw that she was satisfied, he pulled her underwear down and entered her. He was fucking her so good that Lorren couldn't control herself. She loved the way that he was putting it down on her. After he came inside of her, they both fell asleep.

The next morning, Lorren took off of work. She did her normal route as if she was going to work. She dropped RJ off at her mother's house and went to meet the movers at the new apartment. When the movers were done, she called Rico to see if he had left the house. When she didn't get an answer on the house phone, she knew he was gone. She went back to the house to get the rest of her things that she had hiding in the guest room. After making sure everything was perfect in the new apartment, she went to pick up RJ.

17

"Hey mommy, who house is this?" RJ asked as he entered the apartment.

"This is our new home." Lorren said not feeling the fact of taking a child from his father.

"Where is daddy?"

"He's not moving with us. You'll be able to see him."

"He don't love us no more?"

"He do love us, but we just had to move ok."

As soon as that left her mouth, her phone rang.

"Hello." Lorren said knowing who it was.

"Where the fuck you at and what the fuck is wrong with you taking my motherfucking son away from me?" Rico was screaming so much that is spooked Lorren.

"I couldn't live like that anymore. You'll be able to see him, but please don't try and look for us."

"Don't come looking for you? You kidnap my motherfucking son talking about don't come looking for you. Bitch you must lost your mind. Bring your motherfucking ass home now Lorren."

"I'm not coming back. I'll call you and let you know where I'll meet you so you can see RJ."

"Meet you to see my son? Bitch, you must be crazy. I swear I'm going to fuck you up if you moved my son with another nigga. Your ass is mine." Rico said at the top of his lungs.

While he was screaming, Lorren didn't want to hear that, so Lorren hung up the phone and went to fix RJ something to eat.

Chapter 5

India

India hadn't talked to Kevin in a week. She had been blowing his phone up. She had been calling him so much because she wanted some dick and she wanted to know where the fuck Shawn disappeared too. India decided to call his phone again.

"Hello." Kevin said half asleep.

"Nigga, so you don't know how to answer your phone?" India asked.

"Man, what the fuck you talking about?" Kevin asked India, already knowing what she was talking about.

"I have been calling you. Where the fuck you been at?" India asked. She was yelling at Kevin as if she was his girlfriend.

"Hold up shawdii; remember I ain't your man. So chill, I have been busy. What's up? You been calling?" Kevin asked, getting under India's skin.

"Fuck you Kevin! I was calling to see if you saw your whack as friend Shawn." India said.

"Yo, why you looking for Shawn?" Kevin asked, getting out of the bed and wanting to know why the girl that he was trying to get with was looking for his best friend.

"That bitch ass nigga left my motherfucking friend pregnant and I know you know where he is at." India said.

"Naw ma, I don't know where he is at. I'm going to try and find him and I'll call you back." Kevin said to India showing his concern.

"Yeah whatever nigga." India said then hung up the phone.

"That nigga had a nerve to try and play me." India said to herself when she got off the phone with Kevin.

As soon as she got off the phone with Kevin, she called her friend Marvin. Marvin was the guy that India talked to that could make her come without even using his dick. Marvin was a pro with his tongue. Marvin played football for the Redskins. She met him at a club and she kept in contact with him after the time he ate her out and had her whole body weak.

India had just stepped out of the shower when her phone rang.

"Hello." India said while putting lotion on her body.

"Hey baby, are you about ready?" Marvin asked.

"Yeah all I have to do is put my dress on." India told Marvin.

"Ok baby, I'll be there in five minutes." Marvin said before he hung up.

India finished putting lotion on and put her underclothes and slid her dress over her head. She slipped on her heels and combed her hair down. India looked in the mirror and said, "You look great." She blew a kiss to herself then went to meet Marvin who was outside.

Marvin drove a Benz truck. His truck was pimped out and India loved to ride in it. He took her to City Zen. It was an upscale restaurant that the athletes and the rich and famous attended. They had a nice dinner and afterwards Marvin was ready to get some pussy.

He drove India right back to her house and as soon as they got to her house he was ready to get it on and so was India. He pulled her dress over her head and started to kiss her neck and moving down to her breasts. While he was sucking on her breast, her house phone rang. She let the answer machine get it then she continued to let Marvin do his business. All of a sudden as soon as Marvin was making his way down to her pussy, her doorbell rang. Marvin stopped and looked at India as to say get that together.

"Yo, are you expecting someone?" Marvin asked, getting pissed off because he trying to handle his business.

"No. I don't know who that is." India said getting pissed off herself as she got up to see who was at the door.

"Who is it?" India yelled as she walked to the door with her robe on.

"You know who it is. Open the door India." Kevin said.

India took a deep breath, not knowing what to do because she didn't expect to see Kevin at her door. She opened the door a little.

"What do you want Kevin?"

"Damn, you act like you ain't happy to see a nigga. Why you blocking the door? I'm not welcome in your house?" Kevin asked.

"Why didn't you call before you came over? Don't just be popping up at my house. And no you are not welcome in my house." India said.

"I did call, and who do you got in there? Because I know that's the only reason that you not letting me come in."

"I do have company and I haven't talked to you in a week, now you want to show up at my house. Boy you must be crazy. Bye Kevin." India said, trying to close her door.

"That nigga can't make you feel the way I make you feel. I already told you, ma, I was handling business and you know you are my woman. So tell that nigga in there that he has to go because your man is here." Kevin said being his usual cocky self.

India knew it wasn't any way to get rid of Kevin. So she let him in. When she walked back in the living room, Marvin was sitting on the couch waiting for India to come back with just his boxers on.

Marvin looked up and noticed that India wasn't alone.

"Who is that?" Marvin asked, standing his ground.

Not giving India time to explain, Kevin said, "I'm Kevin, India's' man. So I'm sorry partner you have to go."

"Man? India don't have a man." Marvin said not trying to get punked out of his pussy.

"Well, I'm standing right here. This is my woman, so bounce, my nigga." Kevin said about to kick this dude out.

"Well, since you her man, I bought her dinner." Marvin said getting dressed, pissed off.

Kevin peeled off ten hundred dollar bills and handed it to him and said, "This should cover it."

Marvin took the money and walked out the door. But before he got out the door, Kevin yelled, "I bought season tickets!"

India went to catch up to Marvin, but he didn't want to hear it. He just walked to the car and drove off. When she got back in the house, Kevin was sitting on the couch watching TV.

"Do you always have to show up at the wrong time?" India asked him.

"Yep. That's how I make sure you not cheating on me." Kevin said.

"I wish you stop telling people that you are my man. You are not my man, Kevin." India said.

"If I'm not your man, you wouldn't let me come in your house and run that nigga out. So I guess I'm not your man though." Kevin said.

"Whatever Kevin. I just knew you wouldn't leave if I didn't let you in." India said.

"You got that right, sweetie." Kevin said getting up and walking over towards her. He just stood in front of her and looked at her, then he started to sniff her neck, behind her ear, and then placed one finger in side her panties. He then pulled his hands out and sniffed them. He looked at her and said, "You smell like that nigga. Go take a shower and come here so I can give you what you want."

After he said that, he just sat down on the couch and continued watching TV, leaving India puzzled. All India could do was go take a shower.

When she got out of the shower, Kevin sniffed her all over again. This time he fingered India and pulled his fingers out and licked them. Then he sucked on her neck, breast, inner thighs, and then her clit. He ate India so good that she lost her balance and fell on the couch. After her body stopped contracting, Kevin picked India up and entered her. He entered her deep and long. He had her pinned up on the wall and was giving her deep, long strokes. Then he bent her over the couch and was hitting it doggie style. He was giving it to her so good that India was screaming his name and came three times in a row. Then Kevin pulled out and came on India.

When they were done, he cleaned her off and picked her up and took her to the bedroom. As they laid in the bed, he looked at India and said, "You can stop faking now; you know you want me to be your man."

India didn't respond. She just turned over and pulled the covers over her head and went to sleep.

Chapter 6

London

"Where the fuck you been? And I don't want to hear that I been working shit either because I called your fucking office!" London yelled at Keith.

"Yo, I don't feel like hearing that shit. I was out. I didn't break no date or promises with you so why you tripping." Keith said walking away from her.

"Don't turn your fucking back on me. In case you have forgot, we did have plans. You seem to forget all the time." London said.

"Yo, I don't feel like hearing your mouth tonight." He said before putting his jacket on leaving the house.

London couldn't take this shit anymore. Lately, her and Keith have been arguing more and he been coming in late and later. London needed someone to talk to and she went down the list to see who would be available so she can get Keith off her mind. Lisa probably was with Terence, the love of her life. Tracey probably was with Kenny, Danni was with Bryon, India is probably with one of her many dudes, Kim was still down, and Lorren was trying to get herself together after leaving Rico. Since all of London's options were out, she decided to eat ice cream and watch TV until Keith came back.

When Keith finally returned home, London was sleep on the couch. He picked her up and took her to the bed room. When he made sure she was in the bed comfortably, he picked up his phone.

"Hey baby. I don't think I can keep on living like this." Keith said to the caller. As soon as London heard Keith's voice, she kept her eyes closed, but listened very close.

"I love her, and I know I'm hurting her every time I'm with you." He said looking at London as she slept.

"I don't know what I'm going to do because I love you too."

"How are you going to ask me to choose who I want to be with. I didn't ask you to choose." Keith said making sure not to raise his voice to wake London.

"We will talk about this tomorrow; I'll see you at the regular place and at the same time. I love you!" Keith said to the caller before he hung up the phone and went to take a shower.

As soon as London heard the shower water on, she opened her eyes and tears began too. They had been together for five years and now she just got proof that he was cheating on her. She cried herself to sleep and when she woke up the next morning, he was already gone to work. London felt like shit, so she called out. She had a mission today and it was to see who the home wrecker was.

The first thing that she did was call up her crew and let them know that it was an emergency. When all of the girls heard that it was an emergency, they all came to London's house. When they got there, she explained to them what she heard and let them know that she wanted to find out who he was fucking. They all had roles in the plan to find out who the person was that Keith was creeping around with.

Since Kim was pregnant, she had to just follow him and let them know where the meeting place was. India and Tracey were in charge of getting back up, in case they had to whoop some ass. India called her cousin, Peaches, who had two guns that she named Purple Kisses and she was always ready to pop them off. Lisa, Staci, Lorren, and Danni were with London. When they got the call, they would go to the place in all black and be ready to whoop some ass.

Kim followed Keith to an apartment building in VA and watched Keith get out of the car. As soon as he got out of the car, she called London and India, who had all the ghetto chicks with her. She gave them the location and they all met up less than ten minutes later. Kim was so good that she even got the apartment number by going in there flirting with the door man. He told her that he was going to apartment 410, which he goes every other day.

London and the crew went to apartment 410. When they got there, the door was locked but they had Jaz with them, who was a criminal. She picked the lock with no problem and all of the girls went in and heard Keith's voice coming from the bedroom.

They walked to the bedroom and were taken by surprise. They saw Keith behind Taye doing him in the ass. London and Staci were so shocked to see both of their boyfriends fucking. The guys were so into each other that they didn't notice all of the girls standing in the door way. Not in the right state of mind, London took the gun out of Peaches' hands. She aimed the gun towards Keith, who was on the top and pulled the trigger. Not a shooter at all, she missed him by an inch and it hit the pillow. As soon as the shot ran out and it hit the pillow, both guys froze. They noticed that the shot came from behind them and London and everybody was standing there looking at them fucking.

Staci couldn't take it so she ran out the apartment into the hallway with Danni on her heels. Staci was crying her eyes out and when Taye noticed that Staci was with them, he ran out the room naked, passing the girls trying to get to Staci. He didn't care if London had a gun or not because to him, his life was already over. As he came in the hallway trying to explain himself, Staci slapped the shit out of him and told him, "Keep your faggot ass away from me and don't even think about calling me or coming to my house. All of your shit will be in the trash." Staci said and walked away, leaving Taye standing there and she never looked back.

Meanwhile, London still had the gun pointed at Keith, who was scared shitless.

"How could you do this to me? You are a fucking faggot." London said as tears rolled down her face.

"I... I... I didn't mean to hurt you, baby. It just happened." Keith said not moving because he knew London would shoot him and if she didn't Peaches or one of them would.

"You didn't mean to hurt me? You are fucking a man. I can't believe this shit; not a motherfucking woman. You had to cheat on me with a got damn man. How low it that?" London said.

Before Keith could respond to London, she jumped on him and took the butt of the gun and started to whip his ass. She was crying and beating the shit out of him. London lost her mind and forgot where she was for a second, blood was everywhere. Lorren grabbed her sister before she murdered him.

"London, please stop! You're going to kill him." Lorren said trying to bring her sister back.

"I don't give a fuck... that nigga is a faggot; a dick sucking nigga." London was ready to beat his ass some more.

"He is not worth it. Trust me, I want to kill this nigga just like you, but he going to get his." Lorren said.

London looked at her sister and just fell in her arms, crying. Everyone was so fucked up when they left that they went home, but Lorren went home with London to make sure she would be ok.

Chapter 7

Danni

Danni sat in her car for ten minutes. She wasn't in the mood for Bryon's shit. She been gone all day trying to make sure her sister was alright after finding out that her boyfriend was gay. She just wanted to go in the house and sleep, but she knew that was impossible.

Danni finally got out the car and walked to the front door slowly. As soon as she put her key in the door, the door swung open and Bryon was standing there looking pissed off.

"So, where are you coming from?" Bryon questioned her and she didn't even make it in the house yet.

"I'm coming from Staci's house. She really needed me today." Danni tried to explain.

"She needed you? Did you ever think I might have needed you?" Bryon questioned her again.

"I'm sorry Bryon, everything happened so quickly. I had all intention of calling you but, I forgot." Danni really was trying to explain.

"That's why you always getting your ass beat, you never think, Danielle. All you have to do is call me and let me know where the fuck you at. But, no dumb ass Danielle have to be an idiot and stay out and not call and say, 'Bryon my sister needs me. I'll be home later.' I'm starting to think that your ass like ass whippings."

"I said I was sorry, I didn't mean to not call you. Everything just happened so fast."

"I don't want to hear that shit. You know what! I don't feel like dealing with you right now. Get the fuck out of my face."

Danni didn't argue or anything. She just walked to the room, took her clothes off and got in the bed. She was happy that he didn't whoop her ass that night. Danni was sleeping well when she felt Bryon get in the bed. He started rubbing her thighs and massaging her breast. He put his hand in her panties and Danni stopped him.

"No Bryon, I don't feel like having sex tonight." Danni said. Lately, Danni haven't been in the mood to have sex.

"What?" Bryon said getting pissed.

"Just not tonight, maybe tomorrow."

"Oh ok. I know what this is, your ass is sore from the nigga you were with earlier."

"I wasn't with any nigga. I was with my sister and my friends." Danni explained because she knew what was next.

As soon as that statement left her mouth, next thing Danni saw was his fist to her mouth. She could taste the blood and knew he had busted her lip. Then he used her as a punching bag and was hitting her with all body shots that landed in her stomach, ribs, and chest. He whooped her for a good fifteen minutes, and then kicked her out of the bed. Danni was crying so hard and then she crawled to the guest room, where he made her sleep. She cried herself to sleep and asked God why her.

Two hours later, she had sharp pains in her stomach and back. She never experienced any pain like that before.

"Bryon!" Danni yelled his name.

He came running in the room and turned on the light. When he turned the light on, blood was everywhere.

"What the hell is wrong with you woman? Why are you bleeding so much?" Bryon asked in shocked to see so much blood.

"I don't know why I'm bleeding." Danni said weakly.

He wrapped her up in sheets and picked her up to take her to the hospital. When he made it to the emergency room, they took her straight back. Bryon paced the floor for about an hour before the doctor came out and told him Danni had experienced a miscarriage. They released Danni that same night, but told her that she had to be on bed rest for a while.

The next morning Bryon cleaned up the guest room and made Danni breakfast. He made sure she took a bath and everything before he went to work. He called her job and school to inform them that Danni was on bed rest.

When Bryon left, Danni slept so peacefully and she enjoyed the peace she was in. Then her cell phone rang.

"Hello." Danni said weakly.

"Hey sexy, I haven't heard from you in a while." Moe said.

"Hey Moe. I'm sorry I haven't talked to you in a while, but my boyfriend gets real jealous if I talk to other dudes."

"I would too with a woman as fine as you. Anyway, when can I take you out and show you a good time?" Moe asked, not caring if she had a man.

"I don't know when because right now, I'm not doing too well and my boyfriend, well that's another story."

"Well, your boyfriend doesn't have to like it. I'm a real man, baby, and when you done fucking with these lame ass niggas holla at me because I know you are not happy, baby."

"What makes you think I'm not happy?"

"It's all in your voice, baby. If you were with me, you wouldn't sound sad every time I talk to you and you would be the happiest woman in the world." Moe said confidently.

"I been going through a lot and I do need happiness and how about when I feel better, I'll call you and maybe we can go out." Danni said ready to move on with her life, but she didn't know where to start.

"Yeah, I love the sound of that. I hope you feel better pretty lady." Moe said before he hung up.

After Danni hung up with Moe, she couldn't stop smiling. She couldn't wait to go out with him and experience a life with a real man, who would treat her like a woman and not a punching bag. Danni couldn't stop smiling and fell asleep with a smile on her face.

Chapter 8

Kim

While Kim got ready for her brother to pick her up for her doctor's appointment, she had Pleasure P's 'Did you wrong' blasting in the background. She was still bitter about Shawn's disappearing act. She had to pull herself together for the sake of her child that she was carrying, so she got herself out of her slumber. Today was the day that she would find out the sex of the baby and even though she should be happy she really wasn't. Malik and her cousin, Jaz, had been taking care of her and making sure she was doing fine.

Malik finally came to pick Kim up and took her to her appointment. While they were waiting for the doctor to call her back, his phone rang. Then he looked at Kim.

"Baby girl, do you mind seeing the doctor by yourself, I have some business that just came up?" Malik asked.

"Go ahead and handle your business. I'll call you when I'm done." Kim wanted to go by herself anyway but Malik wanted to take her.

He kissed her forehead and left. A few minutes later the doctor called Kim back.

"Hello Ms. Williams. How are you doing?" Dr. Lloyd said.

"Hey Dr. Lloyd, I'm doing ok." Kim replied.

"Are you happy to find out the sex of the baby?"

"Kinda." Kim replied dryly.

Dr. Lloyd got prepared for the sonogram. He put the cold gel on her belly and looked at the baby on the monitor. Kim heard the baby's heart beat and saw the little figure on the monitor and she began to cry. While she was crying, Dr. Lloyd looked at her and said, "Ms. Williams you will be having a baby boy."

After Kim heard that, she cried even harder because Shawn always wanted a boy and now that he got one, he left before he could even find out. After Dr. Lloyd was done, Kim got herself together and called Malik and made another appointment.

While Kim waited for Malik, she got hungry so she walked to the carryout that was around the corner from the doctor's office. She ordered three wings and fries with mumbo sauce on everything. While she waited for her food, a group of guys came in the carryout. Kim was busy texting when one of the guys just sat at her table. She just easily looked up to see who was sitting across from her. It was Quan from the club.

"Hey beautiful, I thought I would never see you again." He said so smooth showing off his nice smile and dimples.

"Hey, long time no see. How you been doing?" Kim said remembering who he was.

"I have been good. So how come you never called me?" Quan asked knowing that he gave her his number.

"I told you that night that I have a man." Kim said.

"You told me we could be friends though." Quan said trying real hard to get at her. He never met a girl like Kim and he really didn't know her, but he just knew she was real.

"Three wings and fries." The Chinese man said to Kim.

Kim got up to get her food and at the same time she saw her brother's truck pull up. Kim walked to the counter and got her food and when she turned around to walk out of the carryout Quan was shocked to see her belly so big. Kim noticed all of his attention went to her belly and she just walked out the store to the truck where Malik helped her into. Not even five minutes later, Kim phone rings.

"Hello." Kim said not recognizing the number.

"So when were you going to tell me you was pregnant?" Quan said.

"Who is this?" Kim asked not catching the voice. As soon as Malik heard her say that, he looked at her ready to curse someone out.

"This is Quan, baby. So you never saved my number, maybe that's why I never got a call from you."

"I'm sorry about that. I got a new phone and didn't put all my numbers in it."

"It's cool. So when were you going to tell me you was pregnant?"

"I didn't know I had to tell you." Kim said.

"Was that your baby father that picked you up?"

"You are asking a lot of questions." Kim stated.

"I don't want to be rude or step on a brothers toes."

"No that is my brother."

"Where is your baby father?"

"I have no idea; if you find him, tell him it would be nice for him to return." Kim said getting a little angry.

"Oh it's like that, ma. He's a lame nigga, huh? Well since you are single now, I want to take you out if that is fine with you?"

"You must be crazy. I'm pregnant and you still want to take me out?" Kim asked shocked.

"Hell yeah, I had an eye for you since the club. So I don't care if you pregnant or not, I'm taking you out this weekend."

"Ok. If you want to." Kim said.

After hanging up with Quan, Malik looked over at her and shook his head. Then he said, "That nigga crazy".

Chapter 9

Lisa

Lisa and Terence had been doing great. They had a connection and she was really in love with him. Larry really liked him because he helped him out with his basketball game and made sure he stayed fresh for school. Terence was such a gentleman; all he wanted to do was please Lisa. The more their relationship moved forward, there were more and more women hating on her. They wanted what she had so they started shit with her all the time.

It was Friday night and Lisa and Terence were about to go out to dinner and met up with some of his friends at a club. When they went to dinner, they enjoyed each other's company and talked about their future. Terence wanted to get a house built and move them to Virginia. He wanted the best for Lisa and Larry. After their lovely dinner, they went to the club where they were going to meet Terence's friends.

When they walked in the club, all eyes were on them. Lisa could feel the stares from women and she didn't care. She knew they hated on her because of who she was with.

"Yo, what's up my nigga?" BJ who was Terence's best friend said once Terence and Lisa came in VIP.

"Ain't shit, my nigga? Just making money and taking care of my girl. You feel me son?" Terence said giving him dap.

"I feel you on making money my nigga, but not on the girl part. Just got rid of my girl, she was mad tripping. Anyway, how you doing Ms. Lisa? Do you have any girlfriends that wouldn't mind dating a thug?" BJ said to Lisa.

Lisa loved BJ, he was like a big brother that she never had. He just would call and check up on her, even though he knew that Terence was taking good care of her.

"I'm doing well, BJ. Oh and to answer your question, I do have a friend named London, who is single now. But she may not give you any play because she just found out that her boyfriend was gay." Lisa said.

"Damn that's fucked up, ma. She probably hate men now." BJ said while Terence shook his head because that was fucked up what ole' boy did to London.

"Naw, she don't hate men, she just hate him." Lisa said giving hope to her friend dating again.

"Well, then little sis hook a brother up. I need a real woman who will love me like you treat that nigga." BJ said.

"I'll see what I can do BJ." Lisa said ordering a drink.

Lisa sat around and drank some drinks and watch her man handle some business. While she was at the club, she saw India's cousin, Peaches. Peaches kept Lisa company while the men did their business. Lisa felt somebody looking at her; and when she looked up, she saw this girl all up in her face. Lisa being Lisa didn't pay her any attention. She drank a couple more drinks and had to use the bathroom.

"Girl, I'll be back. I have to use the bathroom. If Terence look for me, let him know where I'm at." Lisa said to Peaches.

"Ok girl, you don't need me to walk with you." Peaches asked. Lisa had already got up and shook her head no.

Lisa had to pee badly; and when she came out of the stall, she noticed three girls in the mirror and recognized one of them. It was the girl that was all up in her face. Lisa didn't think anything of it, so she went to the sink and washed her hands.

"So, I see you are here with Terence." The girl said to Lisa.

"Yeah and your point is."

"Well, bitch he is my man. So I just want to let you know before I have to whoop your ass."

"If he was your man, he would be here with you and not with me. So, clearly he is my man, bitch." Lisa said showing her ghetto side.

After Lisa said that, the girl swung on Lisa. The girl wasn't that quick because she missed her throw and Lisa reacted quickly by punching her in her face. As soon as Lisa hit the girl, her friends jumped on her. While they were on her, Lisa continued to throw punches. She was handling hers when Peaches walked in the bathroom. When Peaches noticed that it was her family fighting, she jumped right in the fight. Lisa and Peaches was whooping the three girls' asses. They were all up in the fight when security came and grabbed Peaches and Lisa and carried them out of the bathroom. Terence noticed that it was Lisa and Peaches fighting, so he went to get the car. When he got to the car, security had put them out.

"Lisa I'm over here." Terence yelled to Lisa who was looking for him.

Lisa looked at him, and then made sure Peaches was fine and she gave her a hug.

"Why the fuck were you fighting in the club?" Terence asked once she got in the car.

"Don't worry about that nigga. Who the fuck is Ashley? That bitch said she was your woman. So who is lying?" Lisa asked getting pissed.

"Man, calm down with all of that you know you my woman. That bitch was just jealous of you. You know you my one and only. I have never lied to you and I would never lie to you, so don't try and play me baby." Terence said getting pissed.

"Whatever Terence just take me home."

Terence didn't say anything as he drove her home quietly. The only thing that was playing was the radio. Once he pulled up at her house, she just jumped out of the car and left him. By time he got out of the car, Lisa was in the house. He walked in shortly after her.

She went to Larry's room to make sure that he was sleep, and then went straight to her room where Terence was just sitting on the bed watching basketball on ESPN. She walked right passed him to go to the bathroom that was connected to the bedroom. He didn't pay her any attention because he knew that she was still pissed off. She put on some shorts and a wife beater and got in the bed without saying a word to Terence.

"Lisa, when are you going to stop faking and talk to a nigga?" Terence asked because he didn't like when she was mad at him or didn't talk to him.

Lisa acted as if she didn't hear him. Terence wasn't going to take any silent treatment so he started kissing Lisa's neck. She acted like it didn't have any effect on her. Then he pulled her shorts down and went down on her. Lisa tried hard to act like it wasn't getting to her, but she couldn't hold out any longer and started to moan. When he knew she was feeling his style, he easily entered her with no problem.

He was moving in and out slowly, making sure to show her how much he loved her. He made love to Lisa so good that it caused her to cry. When it got too good, one single tear fell from his eye as they exploded together.

"I love you baby and I would never and I mean never hurt you." Terence said as he kissed Lisa.

"I love you too and I believe you." Lisa said.

Terence held her and they slept peacefully.

Chapter 10

Lorren

Lorren woke up in the morning not in the mood to deal with Rico, but she told him he can get RJ for the weekend. She knew what he was going to try, so she already threatened him. If he tried to take her son, she would call the police and everybody knew the police was the black man's enemy. So she got up and got herself along with her son dressed so that they could go meet Rico. RJ was spending the weekend with his father and was so happy. Lorren told Rico to meet her at her mother's house because if he tried something, the dudes who been gunning for him would be able to get his ass.

Lorren heard Rico's music as soon as he pulled up in front of her mother's house. He was blasting Lil' Wayne. She didn't even give him a chance to make it to the door. She beat him to the porch.

"Damn, that was quick." Rico said when he saw how fast Lorren moved.

"I know. RJ, your father is out here." Lorren yelled in the house for her son.

"Damn ma, you look good." Rico said to Lorren while licking his pink lips.

"Thank you." Lorren said while trying not to look at his lips, which were something he used to do to turn her on.

"Ma, you know I miss you, I don't know why you doing this to a nigga. Please come home, I promise I will stop that crazy shit. I can't live without you or my son. I can't sleep, I

44

can't eat. Baby, I'm miserable without you." Rico had a plan and that was to get his family back no matter what it took.

Rico had really been miserable. He had been taking his anger out on any and everybody. One of his workers was short twenty dollars and he beat the shit out of him in the middle of the street. He didn't give a fuck that the worker was his cousin. Lorren leaving him made him angrier and all he wanted was his family back.

"Daddy... Daddy, I miss you." RJ came running out of the house and jumped in his father's arms before Lorren could respond to Rico.

"I miss you too, little man. You got big, I see your mommy been taking good care of you." Rico said still looking a Lorren.

"Yeah she has. She makes me eat all of my vegetables so I can be strong like you. See, look at my muscles, daddy." RJ said showing his father his muscle.

"I see, give your mommy a kiss so we can go do some men stuff."

RJ gave his mother a kiss and told her he loved her. Then Rico looked at Lorren and said he would bring him back on Sunday at 3p.m.

Lorren was happy that the meeting went well. She knew she still miss him a lot, but it was time for a change.

It was the weekend that Lorren was free and she wanted to go to a club. She knew everybody had been going through some shit in their life, but she wanted to party, so she called everybody and asked if they wanted to go to the club. Everybody agreed even though some of them didn't want to go.

All of the girls were there, but Kim. Since she been pregnant she just sleep, work, eat, and sleep some more.

"I'm glad y'all came out with me." Lorren said a little tipsy.

"Girl, it is no problem. I need to go out and take a drink. Kenny ass is getting on my nerves." Tracey said.

"OMG… What is Lover boy doing?" Lisa asked.

"He is so jealous. We went out to eat and the waiter smiled at me. You know he was like, 'So you like him or something. Do I need to leave?" Tracey explained.

"Wow, I would never think Kenny would be the jealous type." India said.

"Fuck niggas." London said out of nowhere.

"Are you going to be alright, sis?" Lorren asked concerned about her sister.

"How would you feel if your boyfriend turned out to be gay?" London asked hinting that she wasn't doing too well.

"Well at least he was the top." India said cracking a joke out of nowhere. Everyone started to laugh, even London.

"Fuck you India." London said.

"Where is Danni?" Lorren asked.

"Girl, we don't know. She really been MIA lately." India said.

The girls just let that subject go and continued to party. Everyone was having a good time. Then this fine ass nigga approached Lorren and he spit some mad game to her. He made Lorren want to have him right then and there.

"Ladies, I love y'all, but I'm about to go." Lorren said to her friends after the dude she was talking to made her ready to fuck.

"Hold up. Where do you think you going?" London asked concerned with her sister, not wanting her to just go sleep with anybody.

"I'm going with Michael and I am grown so let me just go and have fun." Lorren said.

"Well, girl I hear that. Don't do anything that I wouldn't do." India said then laughed.

Lorren laughed and went with Michael to a motel because she didn't want go to his house and she didn't want him to know where she lived either. Lorren was so drunk that she didn't even know how she made it to the motel, but all she knew was that Michael was sexy as shit. She wasn't looking for a relationship, she just wanted to fuck and leave.

Michael started to eat Lorren out and she wasn't really feeling it because he wasn't even alright with eating the pussy. He was horrible. Lorren was so pissed that she just told him to stop and made sure he put on a condom. When Michael was putting on the condom, Lorren looked and was so disappointed in the size of his dick. He didn't even have the condom on when Lorren bent over the side of the bed and vomited.

"Are you ok?" Michael asked, looking shocked because she just vomited on the floor.

"I'm not feeling well. I'm just going to leave." Lorren said getting dressed fast as shit.

"Well, can I get your number and we can continue this another time when you feel better?" Michael asked.

Lorren acted like she didn't hear him and walked out the motel room without looking back.

As soon as she got in the car, she picked up her phone. She called Kim because she knew everybody else was still at the club and Danni hadn't been answering her phone.

"Kim, are you sleeping?" Lorren asked as soon as Kim answered.

"Naw, I was just watching TV. I thought you were at the club?"

"Girl, I was, but I left with this cutie. He was sexy as shit and he talked to me so good that I was going to test him out. Girl, you know I haven't had any in over a month."

"So you left the club to go fuck some cutie? Girl, you a trip. Was he good?" Kim asked curious.

"Hell no, he was some shit. I didn't even let that nigga get the condom on before I was out of there. Girl, his head game was some shit. I had to stop him and when he was putting the condom on, his dick was so little. OMG I threw up at the sight of his little ass dick and his whack ass head."

Kim laughed so hard that tears came out of her eyes. She couldn't believe that her girl just vomited from looking at a dude's dick.

Lorren talked to Kim until she made it home then she told Kim she would catch up with her tomorrow. Lorren went to bed with a smile on her face because Michael's little dick was

the highlight of her day. She never laughed that hard and she
went to bed happy, even though she was still horny.

Chapter 11

Tracey

Tracey had been getting tired of Kenny's ass. Kenny was so jealous and he kept pressing her into having a baby. She loved Kenny, but she was ready to drop his ass with the quickness. Tracey was at home when India called her.

"Hello."

"Hey girl, guess who I saw and he is looking fine ass shit." India said.

"Who girl?" Tracey asked wanting to know who she was talking about.

"Zoe! I ran into him when I was going to get my hair done."

Tracey was shocked because she wasn't expecting Zoe to get out of jail for another year.

"OMG, what did he say?" Tracey was curious if he asked about her.

"He just asked about y'all and that's about it."

"How long has he been out?"

"He been out for three weeks now and trust me he is doing great." India informed her friend who she knew was still madly in love with Zoe.

"Oh well, I'm happy for him." Tracey said a little upset because he didn't call her when he got out of jail. She was quiet for a minute. All kind of thoughts were going through her mind.

She was thinking maybe he has a new girl, or maybe he doesn't think I care about him anymore.

"Yo, Tracey you still there?" India asked because it was so quiet on the phone.

"Oh my bad, I'm here. I got lost in my thoughts real quick." Tracey said snapping out of it.

"Well, girl I'm going to hit you later. I got a date with a doctor and I'm praying that Mr. You-know-who don't show up like he always do." India said.

"Girl, you know you feeling that man. I don't know why you keep on faking." Tracey said pulling India's cards.

"When you stop faking and get your real love back that's when I will stop faking." India said pulling Tracey's cards.

"Whatever, I'll talk to you later." Tracey said before she hung up.

After getting off of the phone with India, Tracey decided that this was the time for her to get up and get her man back, but she just didn't know where to start. She loved Kenny, but she was in love with Zoe. She had to go to the old hang out place and see if she could find him.

Tracey got dressed, put on some tight jeans to show off her curves and a low cut shirt to show off her cleavage. She then drove to the hood that Zoe hustled around and looked for him. She spotted one of her brothers and asked him had he seen Zoe. He told her that Zoe just went to the store.

Tracey got out of the car and hung around her brother Tone, until Zoe came back around the way. When Tracey saw

Zoe, her heart stopped and she felt like she did when she first met him. She felt like a little school girl again.

Zoe just looked at Tracey. He looked at her the way he used to see her. "Hey Tracey, what brings you around here?"

"Hey Zoe, how come you didn't let me know you got out?" Tracey said trying her best not to jump up all over him.

"I know you were with your new man, so I didn't want to be a home wrecker." Zoe said not really giving a fuck about fucking up her relationship with that bitch ass nigga.

"You still could have called me. Where have you been staying?"

"I've been around. Staying here and there." As soon as that left his mouth, a girl came over to where Zoe was standing.

"Baby, I'm ready to go. You said we were going to the concert tonight and you said you were going to take me shopping." The girl said to Zoe, while rubbing on his arm.

"Give me a few minutes. I'm almost done talking to a friend of mine." Zoe said before he slapped the girl on the butt.

Tracey turned red after the girl left. She was so heated and pissed off. She couldn't believe that Zoe would do something like that.

"So, I'm just a friend now?" Tracey asked Zoe.

"Baby girl don't get it twisted, you the one who left me, remember? Catch you later, Tone." Zoe said then walked away to his new car that he just brought.

Tracey felt so stupid. All she could do was get in her car and drive off. She didn't even say anything to her brother; she just left. When she got home she spotted Kenny's car and she wasn't in the mood for his jealous ass.

"Hey baby, how was your day?" Kenny asked as soon as Tracey walked in the door.

"Don't feel like talking." Tracey stated and made a drink then went to the living room. Kenny was right on her heels.

"You shouldn't drink in the midday like that." Kenny said looking out for Tracey.

"Look, don't try and be my father. I can do what I feel."

"I was just trying to look out for you. Damn."

"You know what, I can't do this anymore. You are getting on my last nerve. I thought you were the perfect man to be with, but you are not. You are a cuddling, insecure, overprotective punk. I hate having someone right under me, I hate that you pressure me for a baby all the damn time, I hate that you say 'don't do this, don't do that.' I hate the fact that you are so insecure. I don't think I can keep living like this." Tracey vented to Kenny. She didn't know if it was the drink or her going to see Zoe.

"So what the fuck are you trying to say, Tracey?" Kenny asked getting pissed off.

"What I am saying Kenny is that it is over. OVER... I can't deal with your punk ass anymore."

"You know what Tracey fuck you, you ghetto ass bitch. I should just, show you how much of a punk I am and whoop your ass."

"Whoop who? Nigga, I will fuck you up if you ever think about putting your hands on me, and then my brothers are going to whoop your ass too." Tracey said.

Kenny was so pissed he just left the house; but before he left, he said, "I'll come back and get my shit."

"Don't bother I'll send it to you. You don't have to come back at all."

Kenny slammed the door and Tracey went to her room and gathered up all of his stuff and put it in a trash bag.

Chapter 12

India

India and Lisa waited in the car for Kim to come out her house. They were on their way to the mall to look for an outfit for Lorren and London's party. India always looked for a reason to go shopping. Kim was going to the mall because all of her clothes were getting to small and she needed the exercise.

"Damn Kim, it took your big ass long enough." India said as soon as Kim got in the car.

"I'm sorry India, I don't move as quickly as I used to and it's hard for me to find something to wear." Kim said about to cry. Every little thing made Kim cry.

"I was just playing, Kim, don't start crying." India said trying to make sure her friend didn't cry.

"Am I really fat?" Kim asked with tears rolling down her face.

"No... you look great." India and Lisa said in unison.

They rode to the mall in silence just listening to the radio. Once they got to the mall, they were in a better mood and ready to shop.

India went to all the stores and brought mad stuff. She had at least fifteen bags since she went to every store that was in the mall. Lisa and Kim shopped for baby stuff, while India spent most of her money on club outfits. After they were done shopping, they all went to India's house to get dressed.

"Y'all my baby is coming to the party!" Lisa said happy that she could show her boyfriend off.

"Oh for real? Tell Terence to bring some sexy friends with him because I'm looking for a boo." India said always looking for a man.

"Girl, you are a mess. Don't you have a man?" Kim said.

"You know what Kim. Kiss my ass." India said.

India, Kim, and Lisa got ready and headed to the party which was a club on U Street in DC.

As soon as India got in the club, she went to the bar then hit the dance floor. She was dancing like crazy. After a half an hour on the dance floor she found her girls who were in VIP as always. Even though it was London's birthday she wasn't in the celebrating mood.

"Happy birthday girls, I'm sorry I ain't come and give y'all some love when I got in but that was my song that was on and the dude I was dancing with was sexy as shit." India said after giving them hugs.

"It's cool." Lorren said.

The girls were sitting there and enjoying the scenery when a group of sexy ass niggas walked into the party. That caught all of the ladies eyes; even Lisa who was so committed to her boyfriend.

"Who are they?" Kim asked.

"Oh that's my baby and his friends." Lisa said, happy that Terence could make it.

Terence and his crew walked over to the VIP and some of the girls recognized some of the guys.

"Hey ladies this is BJ, Moe, Quan, Ricky, and Kay." Terence introduced his friends.

All of the ladies said hi at the same time. Quan went right to Kim who he had been talking to and getting close to. Moe was looking for Danni, who was at the party with Bryon. Terence and Lisa went on their way. BJ tried to spit some game to London. Ricky could tell that Lorren or Tracey didn't want to be bothered so he went to the bar and found a girl. Kay on the other hand was all up on India.

"So Kay, what does Kay stand for?" India asked in a flirting way.

"Kavon. So miss India, where is your man?"

"I don't have one, Mr. Kay. Where is your woman?"

"I don't have one. You look to good to not have a man, so you don't have to lie to me beautiful."

"I don't have to lie, boo. If I had a man I would let you know."

They talked for a little while and then danced. They were really digging each other when India's phone rang. She just looked at it and continued to party. When the party was over, India was in the mood to get some dick.

"So beautiful, what are you about to do?" Kay asked after the party was over.

"Since I don't have to drop my girls off, I guess I'm about to go home." India said.

"Well, do you want some company?" Kay said giving her a sly look.

"I'm going to have to pass this time sweetie." India said.

India was shocked by the answer she just gave. She got in the car and it seemed as if it was on cue, her phone rang.

"Yes Kevin?" India asked without even looking at the caller ID.

"Where you at baby?" Kevin asked.

"I'm on U Street, leaving a party. What's up?"

"I need you to come and pick me up from KDP."

"I'm not coming around there. So I guess that means no." India said starting up her car.

"Come on baby don't be like that. You know I wouldn't ask you if I didn't really need you to come and get me."

"Damn. Here I come."

The whole way India drove to pick up Kevin, all she kept saying to herself was, "You must really be losing it India. You really acting like you are this nigga's girl. Come on girl snap out of it." India pulled up where he said he would be. When he got in the car, he had another nigga with him.

"Thanks baby." He said leaning over the seat and kissing India on the cheek.

"Whatever nigga. Where am I taking y'all?" India asked before she pulled off.

"We going to my house." Kevin said.

"I am not driving all the way out Upper Marlboro."

"Come on ma, you wilding. You are spending the night with me anyway."

"What makes you think that boy? I'm going home and sleep in my own bed."

"We will see. Anyway this is Lil Man; he is like my little brother. I take care of him." Kevin said finally introducing India and Lil Man.

"Hey Lil Man." India said then continued to drive quietly.

She already knew that Kevin wasn't going to let her go home that night, so she didn't make a fuss, but she damn sure was going to try and leave. Once she pulled up in front of his beautiful big house, she pulled in the drive way where his truck and car sat.

"It was nice meeting you Lil Man, and I'll talk to you later Kevin." India said trying to escape on the sly.

Kevin got a hint of what she was doing and grabbed her keys. "Don't try and play me shawdii. You know you staying the night so get out the car and come on in the house."

India just sat there. She didn't get out of the car or nothing. So Kevin walked around the car, opened her door, and picked her up from out of the car.

"It's not that bad. You can spend one night with a nigga. You act like I'm going to hurt you." Kevin said.

India didn't say anything as she just walked in his house. When she got in the house, she realized that his house was beautiful. India never went to Kevin's house; he just told her where he lived. She was so shocked at how well designed the house was and how comfortable she felt as soon as she step foot inside.

Kevin noticed the shocked look on India's face and said, "Do you want a tour sweet heart?"

"Sure, why not."

Kevin showed India the whole house and left the master bedroom for last.

"This is the last room in the house. This is where the magic happens." Kevin said before he opened the door.

"Boy, you are silly. This is so nice Kevin. Who designed it for you? One of your girls?" India said showing her envious side.

"No not one of my girls, I paid a designer to come. Besides my mother, you are the only woman that I ever brought to my house."

"So, why did you invite me here?"

"Because you are my woman and those other chicks are hoes. When we are together, we make love. I haven't done that with no other female before." Kevin said moving closer.

"What makes you think I want to be your girl?" India asked stepping way from Kevin.

"Your actions show it. The way we look at each other. You put on a big front, but I know you ready to be with me." Kevin said this time grabbing India and pulling her close to him.

"I don't think you can handle a woman like me." India said loving the feel of being in Kevin arms.

"What makes you think that, I think I been doing a good job so far." Kevin said while kissing her neck and moving down her shoulders.

"Ummm... I need to be number one, I need to be spoiled, ummm... and when you say you love me, you have to mean it, don't just let it come out your mouth and don't mean it because you might get hurt." India said between moans.

Between kisses Kevin said, "Well, if you give me a chance, I'll prove that I can be the man that you will love forever and I promise to never hurt you. So are you going to give me a chance sweet heart?"

Kevin was making India feel so hot and warm inside. Her heart was telling her to give him a chance, but her mind was telling her to just fuck him and get away from him as fast as you can. India for the first time in her life listened to her heart and looked Kevin in the eyes and said, "I'm ready to let you in my heart."

Kevin was so happy that he picked India up and that night they made love all night long. They made love to the wee hours of the morning. After they finished, India slept in Kevin's arms.

Before India fell asleep she said to herself, "Now, this feels so right." Then she went to sleep.

Chapter 13

London

London sat at her desk at work zoned out. Ever since she found out that Keith was fucking, out of all people Taye, she had been a little depressed. She kept herself busy by working hard and hanging with her friends and family all the time. But when she was alone, the story came back to haunt her. Her cell phone rang and pulled her out of her trance.

"Hello." London said not recognizing the number.

"London, I have been trying to get in touch with you." Keith said.

"Keith didn't I tell you to never call me or anything."

"I want to say sorry baby, I still love you."

"Sorry? You right you are sorry; you are a sorry faggot, and if you loved me you wouldn't be fucking a man. Keith please get the fuck off my phone."

"Baby please."

"Bye, Keith! Don't ever call me again." London said before she hung up in his ear.

When London hung up on Keith, she was so pissed that she needed a drink. She left and went on an early lunch break. She just wanted to be by herself to get her thoughts together, so she decided to go to a deli down the street from her job.

She ordered a sub and sat outside to enjoy the cool air and clear her head. While she ate her sandwich and read the newspaper, she felt someone looking at her so she looked up from her newspaper and realized that it was BJ.

"Hey BJ, how are you?" London asked.

"I'm better now that I've seen you beautiful." BJ said really feeling London ever since they talked in the club.

"Oh isn't that charming. What brings you downtown and you are dressed very nice." London said admiring his outfit. BJ had on a nice blue pinned striped suit. He looked so good that he could have been a model.

"I had a business meeting today. You don't look to bad yourself, Miss London." BJ said glad that London loosened up some and wasn't so stuck up like she was before.

"Business, huh?" London said with a smart remark.

"Yes, Miss London. I own a club and I had a couple of contracts that I had to run by my lawyer." BJ informed her.

"Oh I didn't know that. I thought that you were a drug dealer." London said looking around making sure no one heard her.

"You weren't trying to give me a chance at your party, so you didn't hear me when I said I own a club and have two; boy's and girl's clubs that I opened. You thought I was just one of these hustling, black men who sell drugs and kill the community. But baby, I'm a business man. I build up my community, not destroy it."

"Wow. I didn't know that."

London and BJ were having a good conversation. They were getting to know each other better and this was the first time since London found out about Keith that she talked to a man. She had loosened up and gave BJ some slack. While in the middle of their conversation, a figure appeared at their table.

"London!" London and BJ looked once they heard her named called. London was shocked, pissed and angry at the same time when she noticed that it was Keith calling her name.

"What do you want?" London said not hiding the fact that she didn't want to be around him.

"I need to talk to you. I need you to forgive me." Keith said looking bad. He looked as if he hadn't showered, shaved, or eaten.

"I'm already talking to someone, so please leave and never come around me again." London said trying to keep her cool.

"So, is this your new man?" Keith asked feeling rejected.

"Look, man. The lady asked you to stop talking to her and leave. So I'm going to need for you to leave. Alright partner." BJ said, getting tired of Keith in his way.

"You can mind your motherfucking business. This is between me and my woman, so if you have a problem with that, your ass can leave." Keith said.

"Yo, you are starting to piss me off. Clearly she doesn't look like she is your woman. If she was your woman, she wouldn't be here with me. So I think you need to leave before I kick your ass and I'm not joking." BJ said ready to fight.

"Don't worry about him, BJ, he ain't anything but a faggot." London said, grabbing BJ's hand and leading him away from Keith before he beat the shit out of him.

They left Keith standing there looking stupid. Keith was mad because he got dissed and his woman had another man, well that was what he thought. Keith wanted London to feel as bad as he did without her. He wanted to see London depressed and wanting him back. Now that he saw with his own eyes that she was doing well, it made him even angrier.

"So, was that your boyfriend?" BJ asked walking her back to her office.

"My ex." London said in a salty mood after seeing Keith.

"What happened between y'all?" BJ wanted to know even though Lisa already told him about her.

"Well, we were dating for five years and I just recently found out that he was gay. I caught him fucking my friend's boyfriend." London said remembering the horrible moment.

"Damn, that's fucked up beautiful. So is that why you so bitterer towards men now?"

"What's that supposed to mean? I haven't been bitter towards you." London said.

"Shit, baby you carried me like a million times at your party. I just kept coming back because I knew it was something in you that I liked and I am also a determined man that always goes after what I want and you are something that I want." BJ said as they approached her office.

"Oh, well I'm sorry for carrying you, I just been going through a lot with men. No hard feelings?" London asked before going inside of the building.

"None on this end beautiful lady. So when can I take you out or call you? I would love for you and me to continue to get to know each other better." BJ said praying not to get rejected.

"I have your number, I'll call you and then you'll know if you can take me out and you can talk to me then." London said before she left BJ standing outside of her job building.

BJ walked back down the street to get in his car satisfied that he talked to London and knew she would call him.

Chapter 14

Danni

Danni just got out of class. She had been in class for three hours and all she wanted to do was get something to eat and go home and take a nap. As Danni got in her car, her phone rang.

"Hello." Danni said.

"Hey baby, I just wanted to let you know I have a business dinner, so you don't have to cook. You can get something just for yourself." Bryon said.

Danni figured he was in a good mood because he called her and also he was being nice on the phone.

"Ok." Danni said and hung up the phone.

Danni felt like her day was going better than she thought. She felt like she could go home, eat something fast, study a little and be sleep before Bryon came home. Lately, Bryon hadn't put his hands on Danni and she had been staying out his way so he wouldn't back fire and beat her ass.

When Danni finally started up her car, her phone rang again.

Before Danni answered, she said out loud, "Damn what is this call Danni day?"

"Hello." Danni said pulling out of the parking spot.

"Hey sweetie, I haven't heard your voice in a while." Moe said.

"Hey Moe, how you been? I'm sorry for not calling you in a while, but I've been busy and going through a lot." Danni explained.

"I've been good, but I'm doing better now because I heard your voice. It's alright sweetie, I know you are a busy woman."

"You always know what to say to make a girl smile." Danni said while she drove home.

"Naw, I just say what comes to the heart. So since it's been a month since I see your beautiful face, what are you about to do right now?" Moe asked wanting to see Danni.

"Well, I was on my way to pick something up to eat so I can go home and study a little then go to sleep."

"So, if you are going to get something to eat, how about me and you go get something to eat together?" Moe asked hoping she would say ok.

"I guess dinner won't hurt. Where do you want to go?" Danni asked.

"How about that new restaurant in Bowie town center?" Moe asked.

"That's cool because I don't live that far from there."

They decided to meet up in an hour, which would give Danni time to go home, drop her books off and get prepared for her date. When Danni pulled up in front of the restaurant, Moe was standing there on his cell phone. When he noticed Danni, he hung up his phone and went and opened her car door for her. By the time they entered the restaurant their table was ready.

"This is nice." Danni said once they were seated.

"Yeah, this joint is nice. So what will you have today sweetie?" Moe asked so he could order for her.

"I'll take the grill chicken with mash potatoes and salad." Danni said.

When the waiter came back, he ordered her meal and his. They talked about life; they were having a lovely dinner until Danni heard her named called. When Danni heard the voice, you could have brought her for a nickel. She was so scared that she was afraid to turn towards the voice.

"Hey Danielle, what brings you to this restaurant?" Bryon asked keeping his cool.

"Umm, I was just having dinner with a friend." Danni said nervous.

"Oh I'm sorry I don't think we met. I'm Bryon, Danielle's boyfriend and you are?" Bryon said.

"I'm Maurice but my friends call me Moe. It's nice to meet you. I heard a lot about you." Moe said.

"I hope it is all good. Anyway go ahead and continue to eat y'all dinner. I'll see you later at home." Bryon said then gave Danni a kiss and went back to his table.

Danni didn't know how to take his reaction, so she just continued to eat her meal. After her and Moe finished eating, he gave her a kiss on the cheek and they went their separate ways. They did plan on calling each other tomorrow.

The whole ride home, Danni didn't think about her encounter with Bryon. Bryon had left the restaurant before her.

When she got home, Bryon was in the living room drinking some Vodka.

"So did you have fun on your little date?" Bryon asked once he heard Danni come in the house.

"It wasn't a date. He is just my friend and we ate some food." Danni said.

Bryon got up and walked into Danni's face. She could smell the Vodka on his breath. He didn't even say anything to her; all he did was punch her in the face. He punched her so hard that she stumbled backwards. Then he continued to punch her over and over. Danni got on the floor and covered up her face so she wouldn't get anymore blows to her face. When he noticed what she was doing, he continued to stomp her with his boots that he put on before she came home. This was the worst beating that Danni ever got from Bryon. He beat her for about an hour. He had so much energy as if he took an energy drink just to whop her ass.

When he was done whooping her, he looked down at her and said, "I can't stand to look at you right now." He went out the door, leaving Danni on the ground crying.

Danni was hardly able to move so crawled to the stair case and made her way to her room. She forced herself to stand up then she went to the bathroom and looked in the mirror. What she saw made her cry even more. She had a black eye and a busted lip. She pulled her shirt off so she could get in a hot bath, and she had bruises all over her body. It was hard for her to breath. Danni knew she couldn't go to work like this so she had some sick days and used those so no one would see her like that.

Chapter 15

It's Time for a Girl Outing

It was time for all of the girls to get together and go out. The last time they all were together was at Lorren and London party, so it was time for them to catch up. Even though they tried to talk to each other every day, it's nothing like being around them. They decided to go to Red Lobster because Kim was craving some seafood.

"I'm so glad that we decided to go out, I was getting tired of being in the house." Kim said to her friends.

Kim was now seven months and her belly was big as a house, a lot of people thought she was having twins.

"Yeah, me too. I been just working and going home." Lisa said.

"I have something new to tell y'all." London said.

All of the girls gave her their undivided attention.

"Well, I loosened up and told BJ I would give him a chance, but I'm not sure if I will." London said.

"That's so great. Now we all about to have men." Lisa said all happy.

"I don't have a man." Lorren said.

"Me either." Kim agreed with Lorren.

Usually India would agree with them, but she and Kevin had been going on strong, so she just sat back.

"Anyway, where is Danni?" Tracey asked changing the subject.

Everyone said they didn't know where she was.

"Is it me or did anyone talk to her in the last past week?" India asked.

Everyone got quiet and thought about if they had talked to Danni. Then at the same time everybody said, "No, they didn't hear from Danni."

"I think we should go over there and check up on her. I have a feeling that something isn't right." Kim said with her motherly instinct kicking in.

So after the girls ate, they left and headed towards Danni's house. They looked in the drive way and noticed that her car was there, so they knew she was home. They didn't bother knocking because they had a key. They opened the door and it was quiet so they figured that Danni was in her room sleep. When they got to her room, they saw Danni with the cover pulled over her head sleep. India and Lisa ran and jumped on her.

"Ouch…." Danni said when they jumped on her.

"Girl, wake your ass up. We have been trying to call you and everything." London said.

Danni never faced them as they talked to her. She didn't want them to see her face.

"Danni, why aren't you looking at us?" Kim asked feeling something isn't right.

"I'm trying to go back to sleep. That's why." Danni said keeping her face half way under the covers.

When she said that everybody knew something was wrong, so Lisa being the person she was, pulled the covers off of her and they all saw Danni's face.

"Oh sweetie, what happened to you?" Lorren asked. Everyone waited for her response, while Kim cried.

"I'm ok, don't worry about it." Danni said weakly. Ever since Bryon beat Danni it been hard for her to breathe and she hadn't went to the hospital.

"Fuck that, what the fuck happened to you Danni? Don't you dare try and say your ass is fine." Tracey said getting upset that Danni was covering up for whoever did that to her.

Danni started to cry and she started to cry hard. "It was Bryon." Danni said in between cries. She was so ashamed.

"He did this to you? Where the fuck is he?" India asked getting ready to whoop some ass.

"Fuck that, did you go to the hospital, Danni?" Kim asked concerned about her friend's health.

She looked at Kim and said, "No."

Kim being a doctor in training, even though she was going to school to be a dentist, examined her friend to see if anything was broken.

"Yo, fuck him right now; we have to take Danni to the hospital." Kim said.

The girls easily helped Danni to the car and took her to the hospital. She had a fractured rib, black eye, and busted lip. If she would have waited a little longer, she would have had internal bleeding. The doctor told the girls that she would have to say for a while.

Meanwhile….

While Danni was in the hospital, Bryon was at home blowing up her phone. Lisa had grabbed Danni's phone before they left to take her to the hospital.

"What the fuck do you want, you no good son of a bitch?" Lisa said when she answered the phone.

"What the fuck are you talking about? Man, put Danielle on the phone." Bryon said.

"Because of you, my friend is laid up in a hospital bed." Lisa said.

"Yo, I don't even know what you talking about." Bryon said.

"Whatever nigga, stay away from my friend." Lisa said and hung up the phone.

When she hung up on Bryon, her cell phone began to ring.

"Hello." Lisa said sounding upset.

"Hey baby, what's wrong with you?" Terence asked noticing something wrong in her voice.

"I'm at the hospital with Danni right now. And I'm so fucking pissed off." Lisa said.

"Well, me and my man's are on our way up there. You need to calm down too. You know you don't suppose to get all worked up." Terence said.

"I know I didn't even get a chance to tell them. I guess I'll wait another time." Lisa said.

"True, I'm on my way." Terence said.

Lisa, Lorren, London, Kim, Tracey, and India sat in Danni's hospital room. They all watched TV and then there was a knock on the door. When the door opened, it was Terence, BJ, Moe, and Quan together.

"How you doing, sis?" Terence asked giving her a kiss on the cheek.

"I'm fair. I can't complain." Danni said. Then she looked in Moe's direction.

Moe couldn't look at her because it made him angry to see a woman that he is feeling look like that. Moe's mother used to get abused when he was little, but his mother passed away from all of the abuse.

Terence knew that Moe wanted to be alone with Danni, so he said, "Ladies, how about we go to the food court?"

Everybody got up and exited the room, which left Moe and Danni.

"So, what happened sweetie?" Moe asked.

"He beats me. That's why I never wanted to go out with you." Danni finally admitted.

"Why you didn't tell me? I could have got you out of that relationship. The only reason why I didn't take you away from him was because I didn't want to disrespect you." Moe asked.

"I was ashamed. I didn't know what to do." Danni said as tears fell from her eyes.

"It's okay, I'm here now. You are my woman and I won't let anything happen to you." Moe said that while holding her in his arms.

While Dannie dozed off in Moe arms, her door opened and Bryon entered.

"So y'all just friends." Bryon said when he saw Moe holding Danni.

Danni opened her eyes and saw Bryon standing in front of them.

"You punk ass nigga." Moe said taking his arm from around Danni.

"What the fuck you talking about you bitch ass nigga?" Bryon asked.

"I'm the bitch but you have to whip on a female because you can't handle a nigga." Moe said.

"Danni, you telling people that I fucking hit you?" Bryon asked, turning his attention towards Danni.

"Don't worry about what she told me, this is between me and you now. You faggot ass nigga." Moe said.

Bryon looked at Moe then at Danni and said, "I should have killed your dumb ass. You want to fuck with no life ass niggas. Fine then you dumb ass hoe."

Moe didn't say anything else, he lunged towards Bryon and started to whip his ass. They started in Danni's room and ended up in the hospital hallway. Moe was beating the shit out of Bryon, he was stomping him and everything.

When the rest of them came back from the café, they saw Moe whipping Bryon's ass and the guys took off running to get Moe because they knew Moe would kill a person in a heartbeat. Moe might seem innocent and nice but he was a stone cold killer.

Terence and Quan grabbed Moe off Bryon right before he was about to pull his gun out.

"Moe calm down, this ain't the place." BJ said.

"Yo, I'm going to merk this nigga." Moe said.

"Man, we'll get him another day, not today. The ladies are looking and we have to go before security come." Quan said snapping his friend out of his killing mood.

When Moe see blood, he gets in his killing stance.

They left before security came. Bryon was lying on the floor bleeding half to death. India walked over where he laid and kicked him in the stomach. "You punk bitch." She said and they all went into Danni's room as if nothing happened.

Part III

After Rain, Always Comes Sunshine!

Chapter 16

Lorren

Lorren had been out of Rico's life for three months now, and she just realized some changes in her diet. Lately, she had been eating a lot more, sleepy all the time, and moody. Lorren knew she couldn't be pregnant because it had been three months since she had sex and that was with Rico, the night before she left. Lorren got up from her bed and went to take a pregnancy test. When she saw the results, she just sat on the bathroom floor crying.

"Mommy, what's wrong?" RJ came in the bathroom.

"Ain't nothing, baby." Lorren said getting herself together.

"Mommy, the same way you cry, do you know daddy cry too?" RJ said.

"Why does your daddy cry?" Lorren asked.

"He cry because he misses us and want us to come home" RJ said.

"Did your daddy tell you that?" Lorren asked thinking that Rico put him up to that.

"No mommy, daddy didn't tell me that. I could just tell because all he ever talk about is you. When I'm sleep, he just watches me and when he thinks I'm sleeping he always say, "I messed up my family and if you bring them back I promise to change." RJ marked his father.

79

"How did you become so smart?" Lorren asked realizing that RJ wasn't making that up.

"I don't know mommy." RJ said as Lorren tickled him.

Lorren couldn't get Rico's words out of her head. She just continued to think about him. She was getting dressed to go over to London's house when she looked in the mirror and said, "Should I go back to him?" Then she thought about all the shit she went through with Rico and said, "Naw... it took me too long to get away from him."

After Lorren and RJ were ready, they headed to London's house. When they got to London's house, Lorren saw all of her friends' cars. She knew it was time to get advice from her friends because she needed it. RJ got out the car and ran to the house and rang the doorbell nonstop until London came and opened the door.

"Boy, I'm going to kick your ass for ringing that doorbell so much." London said.

RJ laughed because he thought it was funny when his aunts cursed. "Aww auntie, you said ass." RJ repeated.

"Watch your mouth, boy, before I whip you." London said as she picked him up giving him as kiss.

"Hey sis!" Lorren said as walked up to the door.

"What's good? Why you look down?" London asked.

"I have a lot on my mind." Lorren said.

They all walked in the house and RJ gave everyone a hug. Lorren gave everyone a hug too. RJ sat around playing with his coloring book and toys while his mother and aunts talked about what was going on in their lives.

"Lorren, what's wrong honey?" Kim asked concerned because her friend was never quiet.

"I was just thinking." Lorren said.

"What were you thinking about, bitch?" Tracey said and when she said that RJ started laughing.

"Me and Rico." Lorren said.

"What about you two?" London asked getting on the defense because she knew her sister went through a lot with him.

"I can't escape the fact that I'm still madly in love with him." Lorren stated.

"What! You tried and tried to get away from him and now that you got away you want to go back. You are a stupid bitch." London said.

"I can't help who I love London. I just don't know what to do. My heart is telling me to go back to him, but my mind is telling me that you are crazy. But it's something in my heart telling me it would be different this time. What am I going to do?" Lorren said then started to cry.

India got up and walked over to Lorren and put her arm around her. "I think you should follow your heart, sis. Because you only live once and if you love him like you say you do, don't regret not following your heart."

"Y'all I'm also pregnant." Lorren said in between tears.

"Who you pregnant by? The guy you left the club with?" London asked a little confused.

"No… he didn't even get a chance to touch me. I'm pregnant by Rico." Lorren stated.

Everyone was quiet and was in there own train of thoughts. Then London broke the silence.

"Lorren, you know I'm not very fond of Rico, but one thing I can say about him is that he loves you, and I know you love him, so what I'm about to say may shock all of you. Go and get your love back." London said and gave her sister a hug.

London told Lorren she would watch RJ while she went and saw Rico.

Lorren got in her car and drove to Rico's house. When she pulled up in front of his house her heart dropped and she was nervous for the first time. She got out of the car and walked to the front door. She didn't know what to expect. She didn't know if he had company or anything. She just pushed everything to the side and rang the doorbell.

"Who is it?" Rico asked.

"It's Lorren"

Rico opened the door with some shorts and wife-beater on. He was shocked to see her at his front door.

"Can I come in?" Lorren asked because she was still standing on the front porch.

"Oh my bad. Come on in." Rico said moving to the side so Lorren could come in.

"Everything still looks the same." Lorren said when she realized that everything was still in its same place.

"Yeah, I couldn't change anything. So, what brings you here?" Rico asked sitting next to her on the couch.

"Well, I'm pregnant." Lorren said.

"So why are you telling me?" Rico asked.

"It's your baby. You were the last person I had sex with."

"How do I know? You left me three months ago and now you are back to tell me that you pregnant with my baby. How does that sound Lorren?"

"I don't have any reason to lie to you, Rico. Do you want to know why I came here tonight?"

"Yes inform me why you are here tonight."

"I miss you. I love you and I can't see myself with anybody else. I miss our family." Lorren said about to cry.

"I miss you baby, all I wanted was you and RJ to come back in my life. I promise I will never hurt you and I will respect you like the woman you are. I been kicking myself since the day that you left. I love you Lorren and I will love for you to come back in my life. I promise I have changed." Rico said with tears rolling down his face.

Lorren and Rico hugged and kissed. Then they headed to their bedroom and made love that whole night.

"I love you, Lorren, and we going to make it. You, me, RJ, and the baby." Rico said while kissing her forehead and rubbing her stomach.

"I love you too Rico." Lorren said before she fell asleep in his arms.

Chapter 17

London

London was at work about to get off. She had to go to a class that she didn't want to go to. She was in a hurry so she was packing up her stuff very rapidly and when she was almost out the door her office phone rang.

"Ms. Smith speaking." London said.

"Hey sexy, what you doing?" BJ asked.

"OMG… BJ, I'm running late for class. If I don't leave out now, I'm going to be late for school so I'm going to have to call you back, later." London said trying to get off the phone with him.

"Alright I'm about to let you go but first, dinner tonight?"

"Sure, whatever you want BJ just let me go so I can make it to school."

They ended their conversation and London hurried out of the office. She had a test today and she knew she had to be there on time or the professor wouldn't let her take the exam. When she pulled up at her school, she had two minutes to make it to her class and she made it just in time.

London's test was about an hour long and when she was done she headed home. When she got in the house, she changed her clothes and put on some sweat pants and a tee shirt. When she got comfortable in front of the TV, her cell started to ring.

London looked at the caller id and answered, "Hello."

"So, I know your test wasn't that long?" BJ said.

"Naw, I'm done with my test. What's up?"

"I asked you to go to dinner with me tonight, before you left your office."

"Oh I forgot. Let's go another night. I just got comfortable." London said watching TV.

"Look London, I'm on my way to your house and you better be ready when I get there." BJ said then hung up the phone.

London looked at the phone and said, "I don't know who he thinks he is."

London continued to sit on the couch watching TV and then when she got to a good part in her movie the doorbell rang. London took a deep breath.

"Who is it?" She yelled as she walked to the front door.

"Open the door you know who it is." BJ said. BJ was the type of man that would take charge and London was used to taking charge of her men.

London opened the door and went right back to her seat on the couch.

"Yo, why you ain't ready?" BJ asked.

"Because I'm not going anywhere. I'm tired and all I want to do is watch TV and relax." London said.

"You used to running your relationships, aren't you?" BJ asked her.

London just looked at him as if he was stupid and to say nigga you answer that question yourself.

"Well, it's like this Shorty. I'm the man in this relationship, all you have to do is look beautiful and that's not hard for you. So I'm not asking you I'm telling you to go upstairs and get dressed so we can go get something to eat." BJ said looking down at London.

"Who said that you are my man? And if you were my man, I would wear the pants in the relationship." London said.

"I said I'm your man and you always dating punk ass niggas that's why you wear the pants in those weak ass relationships. Now that we got this shit clear, go get dressed so I can take your hard-to-please ass out to eat." BJ said.

London didn't argue; she just got off the couch and went upstairs to get dressed. London never had a dude who took control in their relationship. She was always the one who was in control and called the shots. London came back downstairs ten minutes later to find BJ on his cell phone.

"You look more beautiful than you did with the sweat pants on." BJ said.

"Whatever. Where we going to eat at?" London asked.

"I was thinking Legal Seafood." BJ said.

"I'm allergic to seafood. So I can't go there."

"Well how about you pick the place Ms. London Smith."

"Morton Steakhouse." London said.

"Alright, let's make it happen."

BJ and London got in his brand new Lexus truck. They drove downtown and went to Morton Steakhouse. When they were seated, the waiter took their drink order, and then their food order.

"Damn baby, you eat like a grown man." BJ said after she ordered her food.

"Whatever, you thought I couldn't hang. I like to eat." London said.

London ordered a big ass steak with loaded potatoes, salad, and a starter. BJ was shocked when he saw her eat most of her food. When they were done, BJ paid and they enjoyed each other's company and conversation. So they decided to go back to BJ's house. London really loved BJ's communication skills and she could talk to him about anything and everything.

When they got back to BJ's house, he made sure she was comfortable and they talked about her past and where she sees herself in five years. He massaged her feet and shoulders.

"So why are you so hard on a brother?" BJ asked.

"Because I been through a lot with men and I don't want to go through that again."

"You have been going with the wrong dudes. I'm a real man and I know how to take care of you and show you how to be treated."

"What makes you think you can take care of me?" London asked.

"Because I'm a real man, I already told you that." BJ said.

"Ok Mr. Man." London said laughing at BJ.

They talked for a few minutes, and then BJ leaned over and kissed London. That took her by surprise. They kissed for a good five minutes before London broke the kiss off.

"What are you doing BJ? I don't think I can do this." London said catching her breath.

"I'm kissing you and I was about to show you how a man is supposed to treat a woman." BJ said.

"I'm not ready to do this BJ. How do I know that you won't fuck me over?"

"Because you have to trust me."

London thought about it and leaned over and took BJ by surprise and kissed him. They got heated and BJ picked London up and carried her to his bedroom. He took his time with her and made love to London. She was on cloud 9 when she was with BJ. When they exploded together, London didn't know what would happen next but all she knew was she liked what she was feeling.

Chapter 18

Tracey

Tracey thought about Zoe every day, all day. Tracey just couldn't get him out of her mind. She was sitting on her bed listening to the Musiq Soulchild's song, 'If You leave.' She was so into the song that it brought tears to her eyes. All she could think about were all the good times she had with Zoe. So she got up off her bed, got in the shower, and put on a tight skirt with a low cut shirt. She knew that Zoe didn't leave the house until mid-day and she found out where he moved from Peaches, India's cousin. So she got up and headed to his house. When she made it to VA and saw the big house that he lived in, she was shocked. She knew she couldn't shy up now so she got out of the car and walked up to his door. She knocked on the door and waited for him to answer.

"Yo!" Zoe yelled, and then looked through the peep hole and opened the door.

For a second, they both just looked at each other without saying a word. Then Zoe broke the silence.

"Damn, you look fine. What brings you over here? Hold up. How did you find out where I live?" Zoe asked.

"Peaches told me where you live. You know she know everything. And I came here because I came to claim what is mine." Tracey said. Tracey was never the type to hold back anything. She just said what came to her mind and that is something Zoe loved about her.

"I don't see anything that belongs to you." Zoe said peeping her game.

"Well, I do. Can I come in cause it's cold out here?" Tracey said. It was mid-October and it was a little chilly.

"Oh my bad, yes you can come in." Zoe said moving to the side letting Tracey pass him.

When Tracey walked in, she went right to the living room and Zoe followed her.

"So are we going to get back together or what?" Tracey asked wanting to get right to the chase.

"Whoa. Who said I want to get back with you?" Zoe asked.

"Look, I always been straight up with you and ain't shit changed. I miss you; you were the only person I ever loved and I guess I left you because I got lonely and the attention was there. Do I regret what I did? Yes I do. All I do is sit around and think about you and I can't even remember the last time I was happy because you're not there. You were my happiness and my joy and without you I don't have happiness or joy. So please come back to me." Tracey said looking Zoe straight in the eyes.

Zoe just looked at Tracey with no emotion or anything. Then he got up and started to walk out of the living room, and then he looked back at Tracey and asked, "Are you coming?" Tracey jumped up and smiled and ran into her man's arms.

Zoe took Tracey up stairs and he lifted up her skirt and made sure that he fucked her good, so she wouldn't ever try and pull a stunt like that again. Once they had hot passionate sex for an hour, they had to take a break. Zoe held Tracey close to his heart and they fell asleep. When the sleep was getting good, the phone rang. Tracey answered his phone.

"Hello."

"Put Zoe on the phone." A female voice said though the other end.

"Hold up sweetie, let's get something straight, I am Zoe's woman and make sure you make this your last time calling him." Tracey said in a very polite way.

"What bitch? Put Zoe on the phone."

Tracey looked at Zoe letting him know that he better straighten this out now. Zoe didn't take the phone all he did was yell, "You heard my woman!"

Tracey got back on the phone and said, "Have a nice day sweetie," and hung up.

Tracey turned her attention to Zoe. "Make sure you change that number because I'm not having women calling my man. Ain't shit change Zoe."

Zoe laughed at Tracey trying to be gangsta and said, "It's all about you, baby."

Tracey smiled and climbed on top of Zoe and rode him. They had a lot of sex to make up on so that was what they did all day long.

Chapter 19

India

India and Kevin had been trying the relationship thing for some months now and everything was going smoothly. Even though India was in a relationship with Kevin, she still lived her life. She didn't act all wild like she used to, but she still partied.

India hadn't talked to Kevin in two days and she didn't really care because she and Peaches was about to hit the club and hit it hard. She put on a freak 'em dress and was ready to show her ass. Peaches drove this time and they were ready to go to the club around 11 p.m. When they arrived at the club, it was packed. The line was around the corner. India and Peaches never waited in line so they walked straight to the front and heard the bitches hating because they were let right in.

When they got in the club, they did what they always do; hit the bar up.

"What you drinking tonight girl?" Peaches asked India.

"I have no idea. I need something strong." India said.

"Well, let's take some shots first." Peaches said.

"Ok that's what's up. Now we need someone to buy the shots." India said because she wasn't buying any drinks.

Peaches had found an easy target and he brought them drinks all night. When the girls were feeling their drinks, they hit the dance floor.

India was dancing with some dude, and she was giving it to him. Then in the middle of the song, she looked over to her left and saw Kevin dancing with some hoe. India stopped dancing with the dude and walked over to where Kevin was. She watched the girl turn towards Kevin and dance face to face. India then went and pushed the girl's forehead backward so she could move away from Kevin. Then she stepped to Kevin's face.

"So, I don't hear from my so called boyfriend in two days, but I see him in a club dancing all up on some bitch." India said in his face.

"Yo ma, it's not even like that." Kevin said.

"So a bitch all up in your face and it's not like that?" India asked.

"I ain't say shit when you were dancing up all over that nigga over there like you ain't got no man or something." Kevin said.

"Well unlike you, I tried to call your dumb ass for the two days. You supposed to have been out of town."

"Don't try and play me, baby. I was out of town and I wouldn't lie to you."

"Whatever." India said and walked away.

Kevin just watched India walk back to the bar and order another drink. India wasn't going to let Kevin ruin her night so she went back to partying as if he wasn't there. But, Kevin kept his eye on her the whole night. When it was almost time for the club to be over, Kevin found India on the dance floor. He walked up behind her and slid a hand under her dress.

Then he whispered in her ear, "So you mad at me now?"

India didn't turn around and didn't protest his hand under her dress and said, "What do you think?" still having her back turn to him.

"Ma, you know if I could have called you I would. But you know I never want to bring any attention to you when I'm out of town." Kevin said moving his hand around under her dress.

"So you couldn't call before you came to the club?" India asked loving the feel of his hand roaming under her dress.

"I know I fucked up, baby. Please forgive me." Kevin said then started kissing on the back of her neck.

"Ok, I guess I can forgive you this one time." India said enjoying Kevin touch.

They were so caught up in the moment, India and Kevin forgot they were in the club. Kevin still had his hand under her dress and India was moaning in the middle of the dance floor. When the music stopped, they snapped out of it.

"Come on let's go." Kevin said pulling his hand from under her dress.

"You don't get off that easily. You are not coming over tonight." India said then walked away to find Peaches because the club was about to be over.

When she found Peaches, she saw Kevin looking her way.

"Girl, I saw you out there feeling your man." Peaches said.

"Whatever. I don't even know what you talking about."

"It seem like someone is getting fucked tonight."

"I don't know who that might be, but it damn sure ain't me. He's on punishment." India said.

"Yeah, we'll see." Peaches said.

When the club was over, they walked to Peaches' car. India's phone was ringing off the hook. Kevin kept trying to spend the night. She kept telling him no, but he wouldn't give up. When Peaches dropped India off, India went to take a shower and tried to go to bed, but Kevin wouldn't allow that. When India stopped answering the phone, Kevin came by her house at 5 a.m. India was still sleep but heard her door bell ring.

Half sleep she went to answer the door. "Who is it?"

"Girl, open the door." Kevin said.

India opened the door and just looked at Kevin. "You going to let me in or what?" Kevin asked.

"I shouldn't. Do you know what time it is Kevin?"

"Yeah, it's 5 a.m. Now can I come in?" Kevin asked again.

India moved over to the side and let Kevin in. She went right back to the bedroom, while Kevin went to the kitchen to get something to drink. When he made it to the bedroom, India was back in the bed on her way back to sleep.

"Yo, India wake up." Kevin said.

"What is it that you want Kevin?" India asked with her eyes still closed.

"I can't sleep so you gotta wake up."

"No go to bed. Damn." India said.

He just kept messing with India till she got up.

"I'm up now, what do you want Kevin?" India asked.

"Nothing baby, just wanted to see your beautiful face." Kevin said.

"You play too much. I should have left you on the front." India said sleepy.

Kevin didn't feel like talking, it had been two days since he got some and India made him ready to fuck at the club, so he wanted some from his baby. Every time she fell asleep he would wake her up.

"So since you up, are you going to give your man some?" Kevin asked.

"I knew it was a catch! Why you came over here and won't let me go back to sleep."

"Naw, it's your fault because you got a nigga all hard and shit at the club then going to put a nigga on punishment." Kevin said.

"Whatever, we can do this later on today." India said ready to go to sleep.

Kevin started to feel all up on India's spot to get her in the mood. It didn't take India long to get her hot. Kevin knew all the spots to hit to make her moan and get her in the mood. When he started to do all the things that India liked, he knew it was on after that. They made love until 8 a.m. India was so caught up in the moment that she didn't even protest when Kevin didn't use a condom. When they were done, India finally got some rest that she was waiting for since Kevin came over.

Chapter 20

Lisa

Lisa never felt as happy as she felt now. She, Larry, and Terence were on their way to see Tonya graduate from the rehab program she was in. Lisa was so proud of her mother that she couldn't control her emotions. She was now four months pregnant and showing a little. When they made it to the center, Lisa couldn't stop taking pictures of her mother. Her mother looked so beautiful and she reminded Lisa of her youth. She had gained weight and her skin started to clear up some. Larry was proud of his mother also because he knew she did it for him and he knew life would be better.

When the ceremony was over, Terence treated them to dinner. They all laughed and enjoyed each other's company. Terence had stood up in the middle of dinner and said, "I have some announcements to make."

Everyone gave Terence their attention. Terence cleared his throat.

"Y'all all know that I'm in love with this woman and y'all know I love y'all too. I never been as happy as I am when I'm with her. She is having my baby and I would like for her to be my wife." Terence said.

"What are you talking about?" Lisa asked.

Terence got on one knee and said, "Lisa Davis, would you marry me?"

Lisa couldn't stop the tears from coming down her face. She was crying so much that she couldn't even give him an answer. Then she shook her head yes and he placed the most beautiful ring on her finger that she ever saw. He was so happy that she agreed to marry him that he picked her up and hugged her so tight. All Lisa could say was, "I have to call my girls."

Terence was hoping that Lisa would say yes because he was having a house built for them and the baby. Everything was moving so fast so that it caught Lisa off guard when Terence drove to a big ass house in Wardolf.

"This is all for us." Terence said once he pulled up in the drive way.

Lisa didn't know how to react. Larry jumped out the car and went in the house to look around. He had Tonya and Lisa on his trail. They were so excited. Terence made sure to have enough rooms in the house for Larry and Tonya. He knew her family meant the world to her.

After they finished running around the house, Terence drove Larry and Tonya home. He took Lisa to their new home so they could christen the whole house. They made love in every room. When they were done, she couldn't wait to tell her girls the good news, so she called everybody on three way.

"Ladies, I have some good news." Lisa said really gloomy.

"What's the good news Lisa? We already know that you are pregnant." London said because Lisa been trying to hide her pregnancy from her friends when they already knew she was pregnant.

"Well since y'all already know that, I'm getting married." Lisa said real loud.

"What?" Lorren yelled happy for her friend.

"Congratulations bitch." Tracey said.

Everybody was happy for Lisa. Lisa and the girls talked for a good minute before Terence came in and told her it was time to finish blessing the house.

Chapter 21

Danni

While Danni was in the hospital, Moe was there by her side the whole time. The only time he left was to go handle some business and take a shower then he was right back with her. When it was time for Danni to be released from the hospital, Moe took her straight to his house. Him and his boys went to Bryon's house and got everything that belonged to Danni. Luckily for Bryon, he wasn't home when Moe and his crew came through because he wouldn't be breathing.

Danni laid in Moe's arms, enjoying his body next to hers. Danni never felt the way she did when she was in Moe's arms. Moe was so in love with Danni. He wanted to know all he could know about Danni, so they took that time to learn stuff about each other that no one ever knew about them.

"Danni, why did you stay in that relationship with Bryon?" Moe asked.

"I thought it was love. My dad used to beat my mom, and she always said she loved my father more than anything else."

"So did he used to beat her in front of you?"

"No, I'm a daddy's girl and still am. I just use to hear them fussing and stuff. But, he never put his hands on me."

"Do you still love him?"

"No, I can't love anyone who tried to kill me." Danni said really meaning every word she said. "Now it's my turn to ask you questions."

"Ok go ahead, baby girl." Moe said.

"Why did you get so angry when you found out that Bryon beats me? You really just met me."

"My mom used to get abused by my father also, but unlike you, my mother died from my father beating her. She thought it was love too."

"Where is your father?"

"He is in jail, but if he wasn't he would be dead. He tries to tell my family members to tell me to come and see him, but it's not going to happen. I don't have any parents." Moe said.

"Do you think you would ever beat me?" Danni asked praying that he wouldn't be an abuser.

"No, I would never put my hands on a female." Moe said.

"Who raised you?"

"My grandmother raised me. She told me that my father was sick and she would make sure I would never end up like him."

"So is that why you're so polite to women?" Danni asked because she loved Moe's charm.

"Yes and she always told me that when I find love I am going to fall hard. So I guess my grandmother was right because I'm falling hard over you." Moe said looking Danni straight in the eyes.

"I love you too. Tell me something that I don't know about you." Danni said.

"I never wanted to tell you this, but my nickname is Killer Moe."

"Why is your nickname Killer Moe?" Danni asked.

"Because in the streets, I'm known for pulling the trigger first then asks questions later." Moe said truthfully.

"If you see Bryon, would you kill him?" Danni asked.

"I would never lie to you. To be honest, if I see Bryon, I am going to kill him, only if you are not around me." Moe said.

"Can I ask you another question?" Danni asked.

"Go ahead, baby."

"Can you teach me how to shoot a gun?" Danni asked.

"That's it?"

"Yeah, I just wanted to know how to shoot a gun."

"You know, I would teach my baby how to shoot a gun. I guess you about to be killer D." Moe said laughing.

"You are silly." Danni said.

They talked more and more, and then Moe's cell phone rang. He answered it and listened to what the caller was saying. Little did Danni know, Moe had a bid out on Bryon's alive. When he got off the phone, he jumped out of the bed.

"Where are you going?" Danni asked not wanting him to leave.

"I got some business to handle." Moe said putting on black sweat pants, black hoodie, and black boots.

"You said you won't lie or keep anything from me. Where are you going, Moe?"

"Ok. I have a bid out for Bryon alive and that was the call that they found him for me." Moe said going in the closet getting his guns.

"I want to go." Danni said getting out of the bed.

"I can't allow you to go. It's not safe." Moe said wanting to protect her.

"I'm going, he tried to kill me. I'm going." Danni said putting on the same all black outfit.

Moe didn't argue with Danni. He just let her get dressed and go along for the ride. When they pulled up at the warehouse where they had took Bryon, Moe paid the youngin who snatched him up and they left. In the warehouse it was Moe, Danni, and Kay, who was Moe's right hand man.

"Yo, you brought ma, here with you?" Kay asked when Moe came where he was.

"Don't talk to me about that, it's all ma idea. She got dressed and said she wanted to come." Moe said letting Kay know that he tried to leave her at home.

Kay took the blind fold off of Bryon's face and he looked like he was about to shit brick when he saw Moe and Danni in front of him.

Bryon looked at Danni and said, "I'm sorry, Danielle, I love you. I just let my anger take over." He was crying because he knew his life was about to be over.

Danni just looked at him. Moe was tired of hearing him cry and plea and pulled his gun out.

"Now your bitch ass wants to cry. You should have thought about it before you hit my woman." Moe said.

Then he leaned over and kissed Danni right in front of Bryon.

"You had an angel, but you treated her like shit. But don't get me wrong, Bryon, I'm glad you did fuck up because now she belongs to me. You dumb son of a bitch." Moe said before pointing the gun towards Bryon.

Moe was ready to end this man's life, but before he pulled the trigger Danni said, "Baby, let me do it."

Moe looked at her as if she was going crazy then said, "Naw baby, you might hurt yourself."

"I need to do this. It would make me feel better. Please?" Danni asked.

Moe only wanted to make Danni happy so he handed her the gun.

Bryon saw what just happened and he started to beg. "Danni, please don't do this."

Danni yelled, "Shut up Bryon. You didn't stop when you were beating my ass. So now you want me to stop. Oh and by the way, you love me now? You didn't love me when you made me miscarriage, or when you hospitalized me, or how about when you just was whooping my ass for no reason."

Bryon knew it was over for him. He opened his mouth to say, "I'm sor…" **BANG!**

Danni didn't even let him get the words out before she shot him in the head.

"Damn baby and you wanted me to teach you how to shoot? It looks like you know what you doing." Moe said, walking over to Danni and taking the gun out of her hand.

Then he turned his attention to Kay. "Let's clean this shit up, you know the deal. Baby, go get in the car."

Moe and Kay cleaned up the mess and when they made sure there was no evidence, Moe got in the car and him and Danni headed home. When they made it home, Moe didn't know if she was ok because she was quiet the whole ride home.

"Are you ok, baby?" Moe asked when they got home.

"Yes I'm fine, why you ask that?"

"You didn't say anything in the car and this is your first time killing someone. It's my duty to make sure you are ok." Moe ask showing his concern.

"Thank you baby, but I feel fine. I don't feel any regret or anything."

"Alright baby, just checking." Moe said, going to the bathroom running him and Danni some shower water.

Moe washed every inch of Danni's body and Danni did the same to Moe. After the shower, they made love. During the love making, Moe asked Danni, "Can you have my baby?"

"Yes, I would love to have your baby." Danni said.

Danni and Moe worked on their baby making all night long.

Chapter 22

Kim

Kim was now in her last days of being nine months pregnant and it looked like she could be due any second. Kim's family, friends, and Quan would come by all the time to make her walk or take her to school and work because she was too big to get behind the wheel of her car.

Quan had been by Kim's side ever since he saw her at the carry out. Quan took her to her doctor's appointments, class, and work. He told Kim that he would be the baby's father if she wanted him to be because he knew how it felt to not have a father. Quan's father left his mother when he was born and he came back when he was ten years old so he could meet his brother who was also the same age as him. Their father was a big drug King in New York and he knew his time was almost up so he made sure that both of his sons met to keep the business going. After that, that was the last time he saw his dad, but he saw his brother sometimes. They really didn't claim each other and never introduced each other to their friends or anybody. When Quan met his brother, it would usually be in a populated place and they spoke about business, and then went their separate ways.

Kim was at home eating ice cream, when she heard the front door open. She knew it could only be three people; Quan, Malik, or India. Those three came and checked on her like clockwork, especially since Kim was on leave from work and school. When she looked up, she saw someone she grew to love and adore.

"You're not supposed to be eating ice cream. I can't leave you for an hour." Quan said when he saw Kim eating ice cream from out of the container.

"I couldn't help it. The ice cream was calling my name." Kim said still eating the ice cream.

Quan just shook his head and sat down next to her. He took the ice cream from her because she wasn't supposed to be eating ice cream.

"I really wanted that. Can I please have it?" Kim whined.

"No, you can get up so we can go walking." Quan said standing up so he could help Kim get off the sofa.

Kim struggled to get off the sofa, but Quan was there to help her up. They would walk around the block twice a day.

"What do you want for dinner, baby girl?"

Kim always liked to test her borders with Quan, so she said. "I want ribs and mashed potatoes." Kim started laughing because she already knew what Quan was going to say.

"See you play too much, you are not eating any ribs or mashed potatoes. How about I fix you some baked chicken and a fresh salad?"

"I guess. Can I have ice cream and a brownie for desert?"

"We can share one." Quan said.

Quan and Kim walked the whole block, and then headed back to Kim's house. Kim had her baby shower last week and she had baby stuff all over. Her friends were supposed to come over and put the stuff away, but they haven't made it over yet.

When they arrived back to Kim's house, Quan went to cook dinner and Kim went upstairs and started fixing up the baby room. She was in the middle of cleaning when Quan told her dinner was ready.

Kim was eating when she felt pain in her side.

"You good over there?" Quan asked seeing an expression on Kim that screamed pain.

"I'm ok. It was just a little pain in my side." Kim said then went back to eating.

Kim finished eating, and then they started on the desert that she had been waiting on all day. When Kim was done eating her dessert, she got up from the table to do the dishes. While she did the dishes, Quan had told her earlier that he would put the crib together. While Kim was in the middle of washing dishes, she felt a warm liquid go down her leg. She looked down slowly and almost panicked when she saw blood and water.

Kim didn't know what to do so she screamed, "Quan!"

Quan came running downstairs not sure what was going on and was nervous his damn self. They both were nervous and tried to remember what the doctor said.

"Baby, my water broke and I'm not going to the doctor wet and looking like this." Kim said breathing a normal pace and trying to relax.

"So what do you want me to do?" Quan asked not sure what Kim was asking of him.

"I'm going to go upstairs and take a shower. Can you call the doctor and I need you to pack a bag for me and the baby." Kim said heading for the stairs to get in the shower.

Quan ran to the phone and called Kim's mother Mia, because he didn't know what to do. She took him step by step on what to do and told him she would meet them at the hospital. When Kim got out the shower, she put on some sweats and her contractions were a little closer than they were before. Quan had everything packed and ready by the time Kim got out of the shower.

"Did you call the doctor?" Kim asked counting a contraction that hit her.

"Yeah, I also called your mom. She's going to meet us at the hospital." Quan said helping her in the truck.

When Quan got in the truck, she asked, "Did you call my girls?"

"No. We can call them when we get to the hospital."

"I need to call them now. I'm not having this baby until all of my friends are at the hospital together." Kim said seriously.

"Look ma, it's not the time to be acting crazy. Your girls will be there, even if I have to go pick them up myself." Quan said doing 100 mph on the highway trying to get her to the hospital.

Kim being hard headed got Quan's phone because she didn't know where hers was and dialed India's number.

"Hello." India said not recognizing the number.

110

"It's me India, my water broke. Call the girls." Kim said before another contraction happened.

"Ok girl, I'm on the way." India said.

Quan got Kim to the hospital in no time. The doctor was ready by the time Kim showed up. In the waiting area was her mother, brother, and little sister. They monitored Kim once they got her in the room. They noticed that she was having contractions every ten minutes. They just had her waiting till the contractions were seconds away.

Kim was lying on the bed breathing heavy, when India, Danni, Lisa, Lorren, Tracey, and London came in the room. Kim was happy to see all her friends and knew it was time for her to have her baby now.

"Y'all I wasn't going to have the baby till y'all got here." Kim stated.

"Bitch you crazy." Tracey said.

"Fuck you, Tracey. If I would have had the baby and you weren't here, you would have been pissed." Kim said with the contraction now minutes apart.

"You got that right, bitch, now I hope you ready to have our nephew." Tracey said.

As soon as Tracey said that, the contractions went to thirty seconds apart and Quan was by her side coaching her with breathing. The doctor came in and asked if she wanted the drugs, without any delay she agreed.

Now it was time for Kim to go into delivery. In the room it was Quan and Kim's mother. They supported Kim through the whole delivery. Kim did curse Quan out for being too supportive. After pushing for an hour, an 8 lb. 7 ounce baby boy was born.

Kim named him Xavier Malik Williams. She decided to make her son's middle name after her brother because Malik was always there for her and this was her way to show her appreciation.

Kim was exhausted after having her baby. She fell right to sleep and when she woke up everybody was in her room, all her friends, her family, all her friend's boyfriends, and Quan. Quan was holding the baby as if he was the father.

"You did wonderful, baby." Mia said to her daughter when she noticed she woke up.

"Thank you, ma. I didn't know it hurt that much."

"Bitch, you made a cute ass baby." India said to Kim.

"Watch your mouth, India." Mia said.

"My bad, ma. It's the truth though."

"Thanks. Can I see my baby?" Kim asked.

Quan had gave the baby to Malik and Malik gave Kim the baby. Kim looked at her son and started to cry because he looked so much like Shawn. He had the same colored eyes as Shawn and he had his lips. Everyone knew it was time for them to leave her and the baby alone so everybody but Quan gave her a hug and kiss and left.

When everybody left, Quan reached for the baby. Kim placed him slowly in his arms. He rocked the baby slowly while Kim watched him.

"Hey man, I might not be your biological father, but I am your father. You won't ever have to worry about nothing. I love you man." Quan said.

Baby Xavier got comfortable in Quan's arms and fell to sleep. The nurse came to retrieve the baby, leaving Kim and Quan alone.

"You are great with him." Kim said.

"It comes natural. He's my little man." Quan said leaning over kissing her lips.

"Are you spending the night with me?"

"I was going to go to your house and make sure the baby's room is fixed up. I was going to come back tomorrow morning."

"Ok. I will see you tomorrow." Kim said giving Quan a kiss.

Before Quan left, he said, "Oh when you heal, we going to make another baby."

Kim laughed at him and knew from that day on she had the perfect man, life, family, and friends. Her and her friends went through so much and only good times could emerge from that day on.

Epilogue

2 years later at Kim's 25th Birthday Party

Kim was turning twenty-five years old and everybody, who was everybody, was at the party. Kim's party was at her new house in Bowie that Quan had got built. She was having the time of her life at her party. She just sat back and looked at the kids playing and looked at her friends having a good time. Then she started to think how good all of her friend's lives turned out.

Lisa and Terence had a boy, who was named Terence, just like his father. Little Terence was now two years old, he was a well-mannered boy who was quiet all the time and only cared about sports. They didn't get married yet because Terence was waiting for Lisa to finish school.

London and BJ also had a boy, whose name was Bryant. They named him Bryant because that was BJ's twin brother's name who passed away. He wasn't bad at all; the only thing about Bryant was that he was selfish. He had the only child syndrome. He wanted everything and never shared. London and BJ raised him by telling him he could have whatever he wanted.

Lorren and Rico were doing so great. Rico had done a complete 180 when Lorren and RJ came back into his life. They had a little girl this time. They named their daughter, Lacey, after Lorren's mother. Lorren always said, "If I have a daughter, I will name her after my mother because she is the strongest woman I know." Lorren and Rico spoiled Lacey. They even had RJ spoiling Lacey.

Danni and Moe was the most gangster couple there was. They were so in love it was crazy. Danni and Moe had a boy

114

named, Genesis; they treated him like a king. He got whatever he wanted.

Tracey and Zoe was the couple who fought every day all day but you could tell they were in love. Thank goodness they had a boy because that would have had one rough little girl if they would have had a girl. They named their son, Handsome. Handsome was the son that everybody said they weren't going to watch. He was two years old and cursed and fought all the time and never listened.

India and Kevin both calmed down with the clubbing and India stopped faking on Kevin and started admitting that he was her man. They even had a child. They had twins, a boy and a girl. India was the last of the friends to have a child and she didn't plan on having twins. They named their twins, Kasey and Indie. The twins were the sweetest kids. They were the total opposite from their parents. Their parents had to be the center of attention and the twins were laid back and didn't say much.

Kim and Quan were doing wonderful. Even though Xavier wasn't his son, Quan raised him to believe that he was his father. Xavier was very mature and advanced for his age. Quan and Kim didn't have another baby because Kim wanted to wait until she finished school and also for Xavier to turn three years old.

Kim was in a deep thought when she noticed something wasn't right. Kim snapped out of her train of thought when she didn't see her son Xavier with the other children. She got up and walked over to where the men were at to see if he was over there with Quan.

"What you looking for baby?" Quan asked.

"Have you seen Xavier?" Kim asked.

"Naw, he was over there with the boys. He ain't over there anymore?" Quan asked getting up from the table where he was playing cards.

"I don't see him anywhere."

Kim was about to panic because she couldn't find her son. Quan knew she was about to panic so he said, "Baby calm down. He has to be playing somewhere."

By time that statement left Quan mouth, he spotted Xavier running toward Kim and Quan saying, "Mommy... daddy."

Kim picked him up and hugged him tight. "Where were you? Don't you ever do that again? You almost scared mommy to death."

"Mommy look there go daddy." Xavier said.

By time Kim and Quan looked up to see what Xavier was talking about, Kim stood face to face with Shawn.

"Hey Kim, guess you didn't expect to see me again. Hey bro, you took good care of my woman and my son, I see." Shawn said.

"Bro?" Kim said shocked.

"Shawn?" Quan was shocked too.

If you're interested in becoming an author for True Glory Publications, please submit three completed chapters to Trueglorypublications@gmail.com.

Other released links by True Glory Publications:

Tiffany Stephens

Expect the Unexpected Part 1

http://www.amazon.com/Expect-Unexpected-Tiffany-Stephens-ebook/dp/B00J84URUM/ref=sr_1_1?ie=UTF8&qid=14135 70346&sr=8-1&keywords=TIFFANY+STEPHENS

Expect the Unexpected Part 2

http://www.amazon.com/Expect-Unexpected-2-Tiffany-Stephens-ebook/dp/B00LHCCYG8/ref=sr_1_2?ie=UTF8&qid=1413 570346&sr=8-2&keywords=TIFFANY+STEPHENS

Kim Morris: Tears I Shed Part 1 & 2

http://www.amazon.com/Tears-I-Shed-Kim-Morris/dp/1499319800

http://www.amazon.com/Tears-I-Shed-2-ebook/dp/B00N4FD03C

Sha Cole

Her Mother's Love Part 1

http://www.amazon.com/Her-Mothers-love-Sha-Cole-ebook/dp/B00H93Z03I/ref=sr_1_1?s=digital-text&ie=UTF8&qid=1405463882&sr=1-1&keywords=her+mothers+love

Her Mother's Love Part 2

http://www.amazon.com/HER-MOTHERS-LOVE-Sha-Cole-ebook/dp/B00IKBGWW6/ref=pd_sim_kstore_1?ie=UTF8&refRID=1EFA9EPXRPBSQPZVWHM0

Her Mother's Love Part 3

http://www.amazon.com/Her-Mothers-Love-Sha-Cole-ebook/dp/B00L2SHLNI/ref=pd_sim_kstore_1?ie=UTF8&refRID=1AW831PBNBGAPPP9G8A9

Guessing Game

http://www.amazon.com/Guessing-Game-Sha-Cole-ebook/dp/B00ODST1AA/ref=sr_1_8?ie=UTF8&qid=1413041318&sr=8-8&keywords=Sha+Cole

Niki Jilvontae

A Broken Girl's Journey

http://www.amazon.com/BROKEN-GIRLS-JOURNEY-Niki-Jilvontae-ebook/dp/B00IICJRQK/ref=sr_1_5?ie=UTF8&qid=141341 9382&sr=8-5&keywords=niki+jilvontae

A Broken Girl's Journey 2

http://www.amazon.com/BROKEN-GIRLS-JOURNEY-ebook/dp/B00J9ZM9YW/ref=sr_1_4?ie=UTF8&qid=1413 419382&sr=8-4&keywords=niki+jilvontae

A Broken Girl's Journey 3

http://www.amazon.com/BROKEN-GIRLS-JOURNEY-ebook/dp/B00JVDFTBM/ref=sr_1_1?ie=UTF8&qid=1413 419382&sr=8-1&keywords=niki+jilvontae

A Broken Girl's Journey 4: Kylie's Song

http://www.amazon.com/Broken-Girls-Journey-Kylies-Song-ebook/dp/B00NK89604/ref=sr_1_6?ie=UTF8&qid=14134 19382&sr=8-6&keywords=niki+jilvontae

A Long Way from Home

http://www.amazon.com/Long-Way-Home-Niki-Jilvontae-ebook/dp/B00LCN252U/ref=sr_1_3?ie=UTF8&qid=14134
19382&sr=8-3&keywords=niki+jilvontae

Your Husband, My Man Part 2 KC Blaze

http://www.amazon.com/Your-Husband-Man-YOUR-

HUSBAND-

ebook/dp/B00MUAKRPQ/ref=sr_1_1?ie=UTF8&qid=141

3593158&sr=8-1&keywords=your+husband+my+man+2

Your Husband, My Man Part 3 KC Blaze

http://www.amazon.com/Your-Husband-My-Man-3-

ebook/dp/B00OJODI8Y/ref=sr_1_1?ie=UTF8&qid=14135

93252&sr=8-

1&keywords=your+husband+my+man+3+kc+blaze

Child of a Crackhead I Shameek Speight

http://www.amazon.com/CHILD-CRACKHEAD-Part-1-

ebook/dp/B0049U4W56/ref=sr_1_1?s=digital-

text&ie=UTF8&qid=1413594876&sr=1-

1&keywords=child+of+a+crackhead

Child of a Crackhead II Shameek Speight

http://www.amazon.com/CHILD-CRACKHEAD-II-

Shameek-Speight-

ebook/dp/B004MME12K/ref=sr_1_2?ie=UTF8&qid=1413

593375&sr=8-2&keywords=child+of+a+crackhead+series

Pleasure of Pain Part 1 Shameek Speight

http://www.amazon.com/Pleasure-pain-Shameek-Speight-

ebook/dp/B005C68BE4/ref=sr_1_1?s=digital-

text&ie=UTF8&qid=1413593888&sr=1-

1&keywords=pleasure+of+pain

Infidelity at its Finest Part 1 Kylar Bradshaw

http://www.amazon.com/INFIDELITY-AT-ITS-FINEST-
Book-ebook/dp/B00HV539A0/ref=sr_1_sc_1?s=digital-
text&ie=UTF8&qid=1413595045&sr=1-1-
spell&keywords=Infideltiy+at+its+finest

Infidelity at its Finest Part 2 Kylar Bradshaw

http://www.amazon.com/Infidelity-Finest-Part-Kylar-
Bradshaw-ebook/dp/B00IORHGNA/ref=sr_1_2?s=digital-
text&ie=UTF8&qid=1413593700&sr=1-
2&keywords=infidelity+at+its+finest

Marques Lewis

It's Love For Her part 1 http://www.amazon.com/Its-Love-
Her-Marques-Lewis-
ebook/dp/B00KAQAI1A/ref=la_B00B0GACDI_1_3?s=bo
oks&ie=UTF8&qid=1413647892&sr=1-3

It's Love For Her 2 http://www.amazon.com/Its-Love-For-Her-ebook/dp/B00KXLGG5O/ref=pd_sim_b_1?ie=UTF8&refRID=1ABE9DSRTHFFH13WGH6E

It's Love For Her 3 http://www.amazon.com/Its-Love-For-Her-ebook/dp/B00NUOIP0A/ref=pd_sim_kstore_1?ie=UTF8&refRID=1PYKVRTJJJMYCHE0P5RQ

Words of Wetness http://www.amazon.com/Words-Wetness-Marques-Lewis-ebook/dp/B00MMQT2OU/ref=pd_sim_kstore_2?ie=UTF8&refRID=1FJFWTZSN2DBCV6PX3MG

He Loves Me to Death Sonovia Alexander

http://www.amazon.com/HE-LOVES-DEATH-LOVE-Book-ebook/dp/B00I2E1ARI/ref=sr_1_1?s=books&ie=UTF8&qid=1416789703&sr=1-1&keywords=sonovia+alexander

Silent Cries Sonovia Alexander

http://www.amazon.com/Silent-Cries-Sonovia-Alexander-ebook/dp/B00FANSOEQ/ref=sr_1_6?s=books&ie=UTF8&qid=1416789941&sr=1-6&keywords=sonovia+alexander+silent+cries

Ghetto Love Sonovia Alexander

http://www.amazon.com/GHETTO-LOVE-Sonovia-Alexander-ebook/dp/B00GK5AP5O/ref=sr_1_5?s=books&ie=UTF8&qid=1416790164&sr=1-5&keywords=sonovia+alexander+ghetto+love

Robert Cost

Every Bullet Gotta Name Part 1

http://www.amazon.com/dp/B00SU7KJ7O

Every Bullet Gotta Name Part 2

http://www.amazon.com/dp/B00TE7PSGG

43310911R00074

Made in the USA
Lexington, KY
26 July 2015